MARY & THE ALIENS

For Isaac.

I want you to grow up in a world with hope and not fear.

Mary & the Aliens

ASHLEY GOOD

Foggy Media

PART ONE

"We are all in the gutter,
but some of us are looking at the stars."

- Oscar Wilde

Chapter One

Thursday, June 12th

It was a warm summer night on June the 12th, 1947. The town of Falkland was silent and ready for bed, as the darkness of night rolled across the sky and blanketed the tiny town. Life was silent, except for the chirping of insects and the faint yet eerie howl of coyotes.

Leaning out of the window of the bedroom that she shared with her brother, Mary closed her eyes and took a deep breath, inhaling the gentle summer air. Dry brittle grass that smelled of straw, crisp pine needles, and the faint but salty smell of that night's dinner filled her nose. She smiled, enjoying this rare moment of quiet reprise.

"What planet is that?"

She looked down at her little brother, George, who was using a cardboard tube as a telescope.

"That bright one? It's called Venus." Mary gently twisted the cardboard tube. "Do you see the one that is kind of orange? That is Mars."

While only nine years old, Mary couldn't remember a time when she wasn't looking after her brother. A cherub-faced four-year-old, George still had a childish sense of wonder, which Mary was determined to protect. She knew that the cardboard tube wasn't a real telescope, she was almost ten years old after all, but Mary was happy for any moment of levity that she could share with her brother.

"Mary, what's the difference between a planet and a star?"

"We haven't gotten that far in school yet."

"I can't wait to go to school like you."

Mary could still recall the day that her mother, Margaret, overspent and bought a roll of paper towel to use in the kitchen. She also remembered her mother's second husband, Friedrich, screaming as he threw a tantrum over the purchase. It was impossible for Mary to understand why he would be so upset over something as silly as a roll of soft paper. They worked better than old kitchen towels, and didn't he want her mother to be happy?

She missed her real dad, who died shortly after George was born. Neither sibling knew much about their father's early life, except that he moved up from the United States when he was young, and could always make them laugh. To Mary it didn't feel as though her mother cared much about losing him though. Margaret pulled back. Went numb. Mary was unable to remember much from this period, only that her mom stopped hugging her. Six months later Margaret married Friedrich, the man that would later scream at her over paper towel. Mary couldn't yet understand the world of adults, she just knew that she wanted to be left out of it for as long as possible.

Mary looked down at George who appeared lost in thought staring through his telescope. Almost as if she had manifested it by thinking about it, the peaceful evening was interrupted by the sounds of Margaret and Friedrich screaming. At first muffled, the sound grew louder and louder as they moved into their bedroom, which shared a wall with Mary and George's.

George looked at Mary knowingly, set his telescope down, and climbed into his unmade bed.

While they had both become skilled at ignoring the yelling, the siblings would never get used to the pounding radiating from the wall of their mother's room. Mary caught a glimpse of the fighting one night when she got up for a glass of water. The bedroom door was cracked open just enough for her to witness Friedrich's scrawny and liver-spotted fist slamming against the wall, just shy of her mother's face. Mary was thirsty this evening as well, but she now knew that things like water and going to the washroom should wait for the morning.

Thud. Thud. Thud.

Each thud made Mary flinch.

"Could you read me a story?"

"Not tonight, Georgie."

It was hard for Mary to say no to her little brother. His big doll eyes always got to her. On nights like this, though, Mary knew it was best for the two of them to just go to sleep. The faster that they went to sleep, the sooner that it would be morning.

Mary grabbed Mr. Purdy, George's faithful companion, off the shelf. Their real father gave the bear to George when he was born. Even if there was no way for George to truly remember something from that age, he must have had some residual idea that this bear was from his father, as it was the only thing that was guaranteed to give him comfort.

George gave Mary a big hug as she passed him the dusty bear.

"Good night, Mary."

"Good night, Georgie."

Mary climbed into her bed. The thuds had stopped, replaced by a woman's sobs. Mary took a small portable radio out from under her pillow. On the back of the radio was a small inscription:

To Mary, Love Dad.

Her dad gifted the radio to her in confidence, when he was ill. *No one's supposed to have these yet, Mary. How neat is that?* She could still hear his voice when she focused. Mary turned the radio on at its lowest volume level and placed her head against it to drown out her mother's sobbing.

Chapter Two

Friday, June 13th

It was one of those hot summer days where all anyone could think about was jumping into a cold lake. Everywhere you went, the ambient noise of grasshoppers clicking and hopping through the dead dry grass was inescapable. The only patches of grass that remained green were the few lucky spots shielded by the thirsty pine trees.

Mary stared longingly out of her classroom window. She took a deep breath, and felt the sweet warm air fill her lungs. Open windows always brought her comfort.

Ms. Susan Webb, voted everyone's favourite elementary school teacher for five years in a row according to the Okanagan Commoner newspaper, wiped the days lessons off the board. The other students rushed to leave the classroom, but Mary remained distracted, and also partially stuck to her sweaty plastic school seat.

"Mary?"

Mary jumped slightly, startled by her teacher.

"You can go home now."

Mary hated hearing those words, but she enjoyed hearing Ms. Webb say them. Ms. Webb had one of those voices that could soothe a mountain lion. She could have announced that the school was under attack by the Axis, and it still would have sounded melodic to Mary's ears.

"Huh? Oh…" Mary looked around at all the empty desks. The gross feeling of shame began to wash over her. She was so embarrassed to waste her teachers time like this. "I'm sorry Miss Webb, I got distracted."

"It's okay, Mary. The heat makes all of us sleepy."

She really did love her teacher. Why couldn't Ms. Webb be her mom? She wouldn't yell and scream at her kids or invite strange men over. Mary couldn't imagine Ms. Webb inviting any mean people over at all. She seemed like a woman who enjoyed her space. Maybe she had a cat? Mary liked to imagine that she did.

Mary gathered up her book bag and began to walk towards the classroom door.

"You know that usually I would let you stay in class a while longer, but I have a meeting with Principal Sanders shortly."

"I… I know…" The dry air caused the words to get stuck in

Mary's throat. "I just don't want to go home is all." Ms. Webb leaned in and gave Mary a hug.

"I understand that things aren't good with your mom and step-dad, but they love you in their own ways."

"I'm not sure that they do, though."

"You're a good kid. Anyone would be so lucky to have you as a daughter!"

Even if those words wouldn't change anything, they still felt good to hear. Ms. Webb handed Mary her book report, which had a big red A written on it, with a little smiley face in the corner.

Book bag strapped to her back, and book report in hand, Mary stepped outside of the school. The sun instantly blinded her, but she didn't mind. Sometimes she welcomed uncomfortable moments, as they offered a moment of reprise from her otherwise repetitive existence. What she didn't welcome, though, was being tripped by the only three people that she hated as much as her stepfather.

Within a matter of seconds, Mary went from standing up right to collapsing onto the sizzling concrete steps of the school.

"Oof! And she's down!"

Mary looked down at her skinned knee. She rubbed the blood off with the palm of her hand and began to pick out the few pieces of grit left behind. Three laughing shadows approached her.

Lucy, Don, and Ricky, were, as far as Mary was concerned, worse than the Devil himself. Their torment was inescapable. No matter what she did, whether it was a good day, or bad, they were always there. Waiting. Lingering. Biding their time until they felt it was the perfect time to strike.

"Aww, poor little Mary. All alone without her lamb. Where's your lamb, Mary?" The lead turkey vulture, Lucy, mocked.

Lucy was the preacher's daughter. How cliché. Her blonde curls reminded Mary of the angels on her school's Christmas tree. She felt guilty for associating a demon like Lucy with such a pretty memory. Mary tucked her long thick brown hair behind her ears and dusted herself off. "That's not even a creative insult."

This time the second member of the flock, Ricky, the skinnier of the two sidekicks, pushed Mary, causing her to fall again. This time Mary stayed on the ground. Lucy walked closer and stood over Mary. "I heard she really did have a lamb, but her folks were so poor that they made her eat it!" The evil Christmas ornament incarnate chirped to her two loyal servants.

"How'd you like mutton, Mary?" The original tripper, Don, mocked. His fat cheeks jiggled as he laughed.

And with that, Mary jumped up and tackled Lucy. Mary's family didn't celebrate Christmas, anyway.

"Cat fight!" Ricky called out, while taking a step back and running his fingers through his wavy black hair.

"Get off of me, you freak!" Lucy yelled with disgust.

Mary took a step back. Her face burned with rage.

"Uh oh, we made her mad now!" Don squawked, hands on his hips like chubby wings.

The three brats hurried away haphazardly with their arms in the air. Even in escape, they found a way to make fun of

Mary. Mary watched them for a bit, hoping to herself that they wouldn't double back. She straightened out her clothes, smoothed the creases from her book report, and began to walk home. She only made it a few feet though before she realized that the three bullies were still watching her.

"That's right, you better get home for dinner!" Lucy taunted. "Baaaaa!"

Mary continued to walk home with her head held high. It was only when she was several blocks away, when she was certain that neither Lucy, Ricky, or Don were watching her, that she brushed the warm salty tears off of her cheeks.

Over an hour and several sweaty miles later, Mary reached her house. Standing at the top of the driveway, she paused for a minute. The house, a single level rancher, was old. Even for 1940s sensibilities. The yard and flower beds were unkempt. A rusty old tire swing hung from the lone dry pine tree in the front yard. She remembered her father hanging it up, during happier times. Now the ground under the swing was littered with equally rusty beer tins.

Abruptly very aware of how poor her family was, she dusted off her clothes once again. She didn't want to be envious of the mean kids at school, but sometimes it was difficult not to be. Looking down at her skinned knee, which had begun to heal and was coated in a thick crimson scab, Mary took a deep breath and walked into the house.

Careful not to make a noise, she opened the screen door as slowly as possible. After years of practice, she could confidently navigate her way through the creaky old house without making a sound. Mary couldn't help but think that she would make a fantastic explorer one day. She knew that she would never fall prey to one of those weird jungle booby traps. With her head down, she set her book bag down on the floor, and carefully removed her shoes. Step by careful step, Mary only managed to creep halfway to her bedroom before she was spotted. Maybe she wouldn't be a great explorer after all...

"Mary Louis Schmidt! Get in here and help me make dinner." Mary's mother, Margaret, barked from the kitchen. Mary could remember a time when her mom's voice was gentler, like Mrs. Webb's. Softer. Kinder. Over the years though, her softness had warn away until all that was left were her hard edges. Mary missed how her mother used to be but knew that part of her died alongside her father.

Mary walked into the kitchen without saying a word. She wanted to tell her Mom about her skinned knee, and be comforted. She kept a straight face though. Mary knew that the best way to stay out of trouble was to stay quiet and kept her chin up. Alert, but not too confident, lest she be seen as smug. Margaret shoved a partially plucked pheasant into Mary's unexpecting hands. "Pluck this. And hurry. Your father's been out all day and we need to have things ready when he gets home."

Mary opened her mouth to rebut the father comment, but knew it was best to stay quiet. She looked at the limp bird carcass. Its feathers wilted and stuck to its body like an old dog that had been left in the rain. The bird's melted feathers gave off an odd smell which made Mary think of the hair salon.

She looked at the ends of her own hair. How it hung over her shoulders like wavy chestnut coloured curtains. Rogue pieces hung down and grazed the pheasant as she plucked it. Her mother's hair was long and dark too but had begun to grey around the corners by her eyes. They both had hazel eyes as well. Mary was very much her mother's daughter.

"I can help, too!" George announced proudly as he waddled into the kitchen wearing a striped shirt and short pants. Although it was unspoken, everyone assumed he must have inherited his cute traits from his father.

"Want to help us, Georgie? Go outside and dig up some of those potatoes." Margaret said with a slight hint of sarcasm.

George nodded, and hurried outside like the good boy he was. There were times Mary couldn't help but be a little envious of him, too. He often escaped the brunt of their parent's wrath. Mary wondered if it was because George looked the most like their dead father. God, she missed him so much. As with her jealousy of the three class bullies, this also made Mary sick with guilt. She found that she was envious of a lot, lately. And the guilt was always quick to follow.

Plucking off the wet feathers sounded a lot like tearing wet newspaper. It reminded Mary of the time she made a paper mâché monster in class. While the sound wasn't innately bothersome, knowing that she was pulling out the feathers that once allowed the bird to fly, to be free, made Mary deeply uncomfortable. She finally decided to speak. "I got an A on my book report, Mama."

"That's good, Mary... But your father and I have been talking."

Mary finished plucking the pheasant and placed its body in the kitchen sink.

"We're not sure if school's right for you anymore. I work my behind off all day and could use your help around the house."

"Why doesn't—" Mary paused in thought for a moment.

"*He* help out more." "You know your father—" Mary subtly recoiled at the word.

"Goes out during the day."

"Yeah, drinking." Oops. Mary wished she hadn't said that.

"Watch your mouth," Margaret barked. She raised her hand to Mary but didn't follow through with her threat.

"You know that man provides for us. You don't have any idea how hard it is for an older woman with two kids to find a man!" The words fell out of Margaret's mouth, as if she had played them over and over in her head before. "You count your lucky stars that he came into our life."

Suddenly, Margaret and Mary both heard the front door bang open. *Friedrich would make an even worse jungle explorer than me,* Mary thought to herself. *He would definitely set off all of the traps, get shot with an arrow, get kidnapped, and have his head shrank.*

Margaret instantly pivoted towards the fridge and grabbed a bottle of beer for her husband. Mary found it oddly bemusing to see how her mom handled this task. It was the closest thing to ballet that she would ever witness.

Friedrich was a wiry old man. Old enough to be Mary's grandpa, for sure. He was always slightly greasy looking, as if he had been hard at work outside. Mary knew that he didn't work though. No matter how hard her mother worked to keep Friedrich's clothes starched and pressed, he always looked dirty.

Friedrich sauntered into the house and plopped that day's hunting score down on to the kitchen floor. Blood oozed out of the bag, slowly spreading across the vinyl checkerboard. Unconcerned, he began to participate in Margaret's trashy ballet. In one singular motion he leaned his shot gun against the side of the kitchen table with his left hand and took the beer bottle from Margaret with his right, before popping open the top of the beer bottle with his yellowed teeth. A regular prima ballerina.

"You two talk about Mary's classes yet?"

Her patience gone; Mary stomped out of the kitchen.

Later that evening, Mary and her family sat down to eat dinner. Family dinners at the Schmidt-Johnson household were not a formal affair. Each night, regardless of what was said earlier or who yelled at whom, come hell or high water the family would sit together in the living room, eating off trays and listening to the radio. There was never any reconciliation after a fight. Sometimes Mary wasn't sure if her mother and Friedrich could pick up on the tension at dinner time, or if they were ignorant of it. Mary assumed they kept their faces stuffed purposefully so that they wouldn't have to talk to each other. Dinner was never that tasty.

"I don't understand why Prime Minister King wants to start sending our money over to Europe. They got my boy already, isn't that enough?" Friedrich barked through his mouthful of greasy pheasant. He slammed his bottle of beer down, causing the dinner tray to shake and the drink to foam over.

"Boom!" George cheered with a playful giggle.

"War's not funny! Goddamn little brat." Friedrich raised his hand to George. If Mary's mom couldn't feel the tension before, Mary knew that she felt it then. The atmosphere fell still, and everything slowed down as if the room had been filled up with sand.

"Georgie, go to your room," Margaret spoke in her softest tone.

George's eyes welled up with tears and he quickly ran to his room. Mary could hear the door slam from down the hall.

"Mary, grab a cloth," Margaret ordered.

Mary stood up, instinctively following her mother's orders. But then, she hesitated for a moment. "I'm sick of this. I hate cleaning up all of your messes!"

And with one instantaneous swing, Friedrich slapped her.

The crack of Friedrich's leathery old hand across Mary's soft face cracked like thunder inside the Schmidt-Johnson family's living room. No one could tell if it was the sound, the pain, or the shock that caused Mary to freeze. After several seconds of stunned paralysis Mary flipped her dinner tray over splattering the food across the floor. She ran outside as quickly as she could, pausing only to grab her school bag before slamming the door shut behind her.

Chapter Three

Mary was perched on the tallest branch that she could climb to on the lone old tree in her backyard. The stars were just beginning to come out, as the sun started to set below the expansive wheat field that bordered her family's backyard. If one didn't know what happened at Mary's dinner earlier that evening, they would have assumed that this was a serene scene.

"Get down from there, Mary!" Friedrich drunkenly yelled, "I just wanna talk!"

Mary hunched over and hugged her school bag tightly. She closed her eyes and imagined that she was somewhere else. *Maybe this is all a terrible dream...* Friedrich stumbled around underneath of the tree. He fidgeted with his now empty beer bottle.

"You're useless, ya know. A goddamn fat-head, like your brother."

Mary hugged her bag even tighter.

"You think you're all high and mighty because you go to school? Think you're too good to help your own mother around the house?"

There was silence for a moment. Did Friedrich give up? Mary listened carefully for a moment. She could no longer hear crunches of dried grass from Friedrich's pacing. She carefully peaked around the trunk of the tree to see if her stepfather was still there.

"You little shit. I knew you were still there. Get your ass down here now!" Friedrich paused for a moment. "Your Mom told me to bring you in to clean up your dinner mess, and that's what I'm going to do!" And with that, he threw the empty beer bottle at Mary.

Mary ducked as the bottle hit the tree. It shattered; the shower of green glass just barely missed her face. Mary took her portable radio out of her school bag and traced her fingers around the inscription that her real father wrote. She turned it up as loudly as it would go and wrapped around it like a safety blanket. Few things in life were as certain as Mary knowing that she would be up there for some time. She figured that she might as well listen to a radio show instead of Friedrich's drunken obscenities.

Mary woke up sometime later, still clutching the radio. The sun had fully set behind the field, and the world was pitch black. She peered around the thick old tree trunk and breathed a sigh of relief to see that Friedrich had gone back into the house. Mary turned the radio off, as the current channel was only receiving static. Everything was silent except for the sound of crickets. *I'm probably the only one still awake in the entire town,* Mary thought to herself.

Just as she prepared to lower herself off the tree branch, a bright blue glow streaked across the sky. *Was it a meteor? An asteroid?* Mary wasn't far enough in school to know the difference yet. Refreshed from her nap and not ready to go home, she decided to chase the glow down and find out for sure what it was. Gripping the rough branch, she lowered herself back to ground. Mary brushed herself off and looked around once more to make sure she wasn't being watched. Now that the coast was clear, it was time for Mary to go on an adventure!

Chapter Four

Saturday, June 14th

The moon was so big and bright that night that it illuminated Mary's path as she sprinted across the neighbouring field. The number of gopher holes that Mary had to dodge reminded her of track class. *Run, run, jump, run, dodge...* Mary wasn't sure what she saw crash in the distance, but she knew she wanted to be the first one there.

Winded and sweaty, Mary finally reached the forest at the end of the field. As bright as the moon was that night, it wasn't strong enough to permeate the thick brush. Mary was always prepared, though. She dug through her school bag and pulled out her clunky old flashlight, another old gift from her father. Mary gave it a shake and listened to the rattle of the bulky D batteries. She wasn't certain that the flashlight would have enough of a charge to last her through the night, but was determined to trudge ahead regardless. Mary looked back over her shoulder at the field before taking a deep breath and stepping into the darkness. The forest was creepy, even for someone as brave as Mary.

Was that howl from a coyote? Or a wolf? Wendigo? Sasquatch? Mary needed something to take her mind off her surroundings. She took out her portable radio. Most stations went quiet at night, but Mary knew that without fail she could always listen to a late-night talk show. The shows were not aimed at children, but Mary knew well enough which words she could and couldn't use at home. At least if she played it loudly enough, the banter would keep the wild animals away.

After an arduous trek through the woods, Mary had at last reached the other side. The forest bordered the local quarry. Thankfully the moon was shining brightly enough that the edge was visible. Mary gingerly pushed a small rock over the embankment. *That could have been quite the fall...* The moon shone brightly over the quarry revealing the result of the mysterious glow the Mary was chasing. A real-life spaceship!

The ship was much flimsier looking than the ones she had imagined; it looked like it was made from aluminum foil. *No wonder it crashed,* Mary thought to herself. She couldn't believe her eyes, which began to itch from all the dust in the air. Smoke plumes radiated out of the center of the wrecked flying saucer.

Suddenly, Mary began to hear voices coming from somewhere other than the airwaves. She turned off the radio and crouched behind a boulder. Peering over the top of the rock, Mary spotted two teenage boys playing amongst the pieces of the crashed ship. She turned away and hid.

"Can ya believe this thing?" Gary hollered as he carelessly tossed around a large strange looking gun.

"Come on, stop it," his friend Phillip begged, as he tried to keep a careful distance.

"Aw come on. I'm just having a gas!" A squirrel ran by, catching the irresponsible boy's eye. "Ooh, free dinner..." The boy raised up the plastic looking gun and aimed at the squirrel the best he could.

"Come on, Gary. It's just a little—"

Expecting a bullet to fire and not a massive energy beam, the force of the weapon's blast knocked Gary off balance. He spun around, ray gun still firing. And with that, Gary's childhood best friend turned into a pile of pink goo. The gelatinous figure, formally known as Phillip, collapsed and splattered everywhere. The backsplash just barely missed the terrified squirrel.

"PHILLIP!" Gary screamed. After a moment of pure terror, he dropped the ray gun and ran away as quickly as he could.

Having missed the commotion while hiding behind the boulder, Mary decided she might as well go in for a closer look now that things had quieted down. She lowered her feet over the side of the quarry and slid down. *Hey, that was kind of fun.* Mary coughed as the dust from the side of the quarry filled her lungs.

The nearly liquified squirrel watched Mary as she walked through the piles of wreckage and towards the slimy pile of Phillip. Mary stared at the goop curiously, and then the ray gun. *Pile of goop. Ray gun. Pile of goop. Ray gun...* She looked from one to the other before cautiously poking at the pink pile of mucilaginous mess. She debated tasting it, but something in her gut told her that was probably a bad idea.

Mary froze. She could hear the faint crunching of car tires driving across the gravel road into the quarry. The squirrel scurried away, and she realized that she should do the same. She looked around, trying to memorize as much detail as she could of the alien debris. Suddenly, the approaching cars turned on their beacon lights, revealing that they were police cars. Mary hastily grabbed the strange gun from the ground and shoved it into her book bag, before hurrying back up the side of the quarry and into the pitch-black forest.

With only late-night talk radio for company, she sat crossed legged alone on the floor of the shadowy forest. The moss tickled the backs of her legs ever so slightly. At least, she hoped it was the moss and not something with legs. By now her eyes had mostly adjusted to the darkness. Sure, the flash-light could have been a big help, but no matter how scary the forest was Mary was more afraid of police finding her. Her family didn't have a very good relationship the authorities, especially with the local British Columbia Provincial Police.

Mary stared at her book bag intently. She took a deep breath, inhaling the sweet smells of lichen and pine, and un-did the claps on the canvas sack. Reaching nervously into the bag, Mary gingerly picked up the ray gun. It was surprisingly heavy for its small size. The gun was glowing faintly, but hopefully not enough to draw attention. She slowly lifted it up to her eye, targeting a lone pine cone that was hanging from a distant branch, just like she had seen Friedrich do while hunting. Mary inhaled deeply to steady herself. Unsure of what to expect, she placed her finger on what looked like the trigger and squeezed gently.

The ray gun charged up briefly before shooting a massive energy bolt out into the forest. The alarming strength of the shot knocked Mary backwards and into the base of a birch tree. Ouch. After the initial stunned feeling wore off, she hoped that the stray energy bolt didn't hit anything in the sky, because she most certainly missed the targeted pine cone.

Several hours later as the sun was beginning to rise, Mary made her way back to her house. Not wanting to wake her mother, or worse, Friedrich, Mary slowly opened the screen door and twisted the handle of the front door as carefully as she could. Friedrich was fast asleep on the couch. He looked peaceful, except for muttering random words in German as he slept. Mary only recognized the word "scheiße." Drinking all day and yelling at children apparently took a lot out of him.

Mary walked cautiously down the hallway, stepping deliberately on just the right spots so as not to make the floorboards creak. On the way to her bedroom, Mary noticed that her mother's bedroom door was open. She paused for a moment and took in the rare view of her mom in a state of rest. She looked so serene.

Finally reaching her own room, Mary placed her school bag next to the bed, slowly laid down, and closed her eyes.

"Mary?" George groggily asked. "Hey Georgie."

"Where'd you go?"

"I just had to leave for a while," Mary spoke while just on the cusp of sleep.

George paused for a moment, also mid sleep. "I don't like it when you're gone."

"I'm sorry Georgie," Mary spoke carefully.

She could feel a knot forming in her throat and tried desperately not to cry. Mary was a tough kid, but upsetting her brother was a sure-fire way to make her feel weak.

"I get scared."

Mary rolled on her side and faced her brother. *Stay strong, he can't see you upset.* "I don't like leaving you alone here, either."

"Can I come with you, the next time you leave?"

Mary remained silent and waited for George to fall back asleep. She didn't want to lie to him.

Chapter Five

Saturday, June 14th

It was a beautiful morning. Although the sun had just come up, the summer heat was already beginning to radiate through the windows. Having only gone to sleep a couple hours earlier, Mary started to roll over, trying to get the sun out of her eyes, when a small dark figure stood in front of her blocking the sun. She began to drift back to sleep, before she realized that her little brother was staring at her.

"What is it, Georgie?"

"Mom and Bad Daddy are at it again." Not many toddlers had as much practice at sounding exasperated as little George.

"But it's so early..."

"They're talking something about wanting to go hunting... I don't want to go hunting, Mary. Bad Daddy scares me. I, I can garden though!"

Mary bolted out of her bedroom. At least she didn't have to worry about changing out of her pajamas, since she was still in yesterday's clothes. She hurried towards the sound of her parents fighting in the kitchen. As she got closer to the kitchen, she couldn't help but think that her parent's shadows looked like a twisted shadow puppet show.

"I told you, George is too young to go out shootin' all weekend. And Mary's got homework," Margaret barked.

While Mary wasn't happy that her mom was yelling, she was grateful that it sounded like she was defending Mary this time.

"I thought we decided that she wasn't going back to school in the fall? Isn't that what we talked about?" Friedrich yelled, determined to one up Margaret. "You know, I do a whole lotta talking, but no one listens!"

Mary decided to return the favour and defend her mother. "Leave her alone!" Mary screeched in the way that only a little girl could.

"Jesus girl, don't start with me this early. Grab your things. We're gonna go hunting," Friedrich retorted in a surprisingly nonchalant way. That was the thing about Friedrich, he could go from angry to calm and back again faster than you could say bonkers.

Mary looked to Margaret for assurance.

"Just go with him," she said while averting her gaze, unable to look her daughter in the eyes.

One hour later Mary and Friedrich were sitting in the dried-out field behind their house. Friedrich was perched in a lawn chair, while Mary sat on the ground, using her book bag as a seat. The sun had become even more intense as the morning went on, and Mary wanted nothing more than to go back indoors.

Friedrich leaned over and retrieved a beer from his backpack. The can released a satisfying hiss as Friedrich cracked it open with his teeth. It was marvelous to Mary that such yellowed teeth could still be so strong. Maybe she didn't need to brush her teeth every day after all?

"You've got to learn to provide for this family," Friedrich said to Mary, while staring out into the field.

"I can fish?"

"What, you expect your family to eat fish all day like one of the Japanese? Bah! You should be tried for treason," Friedrich rambled.

Ignoring her drunken stepfather, Mary unzipped her school bag and looked inside. She had brought a few books, in case Friedrich decided to take a nap and she had time, as well as her trusty radio, which had the ray gun tucked behind.

"No one wants to hire women, nor should they. But that doesn't mean you can't learn basic skills to feed your family," Friedrich trailed off as he picked up a long-barreled gun and pointed it towards whatever it was that he had been staring at, all without leaving his chair.

"I could just go to the grocery store, like a normal person?"
"You think they just give you food for free? Besides, people that can't hunt are pansies! A bunch of fruit salads if you ask me. No sense in buying food when there's perfectly good free meat in your own backyard..."

Just then, a gopher popped up from the spot that Friedrich had been fixated on. "There's one! Get it!" Friedrich whisper-yelled, as he passed Mary the gun.

"I really don't want to…"

"Oh, for Christ's sake, kid." Friedrich took the gun back from Mary and fired it at the unsuspecting gopher. The rodent exploded, like a blood-filled water balloon. "Whoopsie daisy! I forgot I was usin' the heavy artillery. You'll wanna use a pellet gun for gophers, or a rifle if you're feeling ambitious."

Friedrich leaned over and picked up another long-barreled gun. Mary hoped it was the correct gun this time; Friedrich owned so many, she understood how it could be confusing. Friedrich creakily got up from his lawn chair and stood over Mary with a gun in each hand, swaying slightly as his breakfast beers began to hit him. "Shot guns are best for things like deer, or people," Friedrich said while gesturing with the gun he used to blow up the gopher. "While pellet guns are for little critters, like vermin or birds," he gestured with what he believed, and Mary hoped, to be a pellet gun.

"Yes-sir-ee, there is a proper gun for each of God's creatures," Friedrich spoke longingly, while lining up another gopher in the pellet gun's sight. Ready, aim, fire. Rather than exploding, this gopher let out a sickening albeit brief squeal. "Well, whatcha waiting for? Go get it."

Mary walked into the dry field, about five yards, to retrieve the dead gopher. It was strange to her that this creature was alive just a minute ago, and now here it was. Dead. She understood that everything must eventually die, and that this was the circle of life, but it was still a morose feeling. Mary stared at it for a moment, before picking up the gopher's lifeless body. It was still warm. Mary wasn't sure if it was because of the hot sun or not.

"You. Gotta. Be. Useful!" Friedrich commanded as he slapped Mary on the back of the head; his blows punctuating his words. His already limited patience had clearly worn thin. Mary passed her stepfather the gopher, which he quickly and haphazardly gutted, before placing it in his bloodied old hunting sack. "I swear, everyone in this family is goddamn deaf and dumb. But not in the good way," he mumbled while walking back to his chair.

Once seated Friedrich turned to get another beer, which he proceeded to again crack open with his teeth. Mary thought he would probably pass out soon, so she might as well read. *He killed the gopher, he made whatever point he was trying to make...* She took the book out of her bag and began to read. As soon as she got to the second page, Friedrich spotted the book out of the corner of his eye.

"Put that away. I need your eyes on the field," Friedrich barked as he awkwardly kicked the book out of Mary's hands without leaving his chair. The book landed face down in the dirt just out of Mary's grasp. "School is useless. That's why you're not going back for fourth grade..."

Mary could feel that damn knot forming once again in her throat.

"I told you, you're staying home with your Mom from now on," Friedrich said while finally standing up, as if he was a king making a proclamation. "No women of mine are going to waste their time on useless hobbies like school. I lost my son in the war because he was weak—should'a spent time train-ing instead of reading. I'm not having another weak family!" Friedrich yelled as he kicked over his folding chair throne. He stood over Mary, who was slowly backing up across the dirt.

"Stop cowering!" Friedrich booted Mary in the shins. Tired of being hit, Mary scrambled to her feet and grabbed the ray gun out of her bag. She aimed it at Friedrich.

"Don't touch me."

"Ooh, what's that? A little squirt gun? Got yourself a Water Pistol?" The arrogant false king mocked, while continuing to approach Mary.

"Stay back. I'm serious," Mary demanded. "Are you threat-ening me?"

"You keep hurting Mom and George. I'm not going to take it, anymore!"

"Watch your mouth you ungrateful little—"

Before Friedrich could finish cussing out Mary, she fired the ray gun. Friedrich was immediately turned into a large tower of pink goo. As if it was his final attempt to upset her one last time, the Friedrich-shaped tower of goo collapsed onto Mary, splattering everywhere as if someone had dropped a massive aspic salad. The goo coated Mary from head to toe and hit everything within a ten-foot radius: the discarded book, the folding chair, and even an onlooking gopher.

Mary stood in wide-eyed shock for what felt like forever before wiping a huge glob of the disgusting gunk from her face and flicking it onto the ground.

Chapter Six

Mary stood on the front steps of her house. She looked down at her clothes, which were still coated in a disgusting pink goo. While it looked like she was coated in a gelatinous dessert, it most certainly didn't smell that way. The smell was metallic, which makes sense since the goop was made up of Mary's melted stepfather… Mary knew she was going to get in trouble for this. She took a deep breath to prepare herself for her encounter with her mom and gagged from the smell.

"MARY! What in high hell happened to you?" Margaret screamed.

Mary had hoped she could make her to way to the washroom to get cleaned up before telling her mother what happened, but not everything goes according to plan. Her mother sprinted over from the kitchen with a tea towel and immediately began cleaning Mary's face. She sort of enjoyed the attention but couldn't help but think that her mother just didn't want Mary to get the floor dirty.

"What did you and your father get up to?" Margaret asked while crouching down to Mary's level.

"I…" Mary was hesitant to admit that she shot her step-father with a ray gun; it wasn't exactly an easy topic for any-one, let alone a nine-year-old, to bring up. "I got sick of him hurting us, Mama."

Margaret stopped picking pieces of her husband out of Mary's hair and looked her daughter straight in the eyes, "What do you mean?"

"That man you married. I got tired of him always hittin' me." This time it was Mary who couldn't look her mother in the eyes. She felt guilty, even though she was protecting her-self. What was this feeling?

Margaret sprang to her feet. "What did you do, Mary?"

"I uh, I found this thing the other night. I kept it, because it looked neat," Mary took the ray gun out of her bag. "When he tried to touch me again today, I used it."

Margaret began to back away from Mary, trembling. "What did you do to your father?"

"Stop calling him that!" Mary hollered, while still looking at the ground.

"What did you do?!" Margaret shrieked.

"I used this," Mary held up the ray gun, as if it was any old trinket. "It turned him into gelatin," she said as she flicked a glob of Friedrich onto the floor.

Margaret had already backed up as far as she could and now had her back up against the wall. Mary couldn't understand why her mom was acting this way. "Mom, it's okay! Now he can't hurt us anymore! He's just Jell-O!"

George cautiously walked into the room. "Is Bad Daddy gone?"

"George, go to your room!" Margaret screamed at the confused toddler.

George looked to Mary for approval, the confusion in his little face mirroring his sister's internal feelings.

"It's okay. Listen to Mom."

"It is absolutely not okay! My baby is a killer! A lunatic!" Margaret choked out. She had started to cry.

"But he always hurt you!" Mary shouted, confounded.

"So what? That man provided for us! How'd you think we keep a roof over our heads? That man paid for everything!"

Mary looked around at her family's decrepit house. "He wasn't doing a good job of it though—"

Before she could finish her sentence, Margaret leaned in and slapped her.

Crack.

"You think you know what's good for this family, huh? Get out of here then! Leave!"

"But Mama, I was just protecting us—"

"Leave!" Margaret yelled at the top of her lungs.

"You're lucky I don't call the authorities on you!" Margaret added as Mary ran away, the screen door swinging behind her.

Once outside, Mary snuck around to the other side of the house. She hopped up and tapped on her bedroom window to get George's attention. "Georgie! Georgie!" Mary whisper-yelled as loudly as she could between jumps.George, always the loyal brother, opened the window.

"What happened Mary? Did you say Bad Dad is gone now?"

"Yes, he's gone. He's… Not coming back."

"Why is Mom mad then?"

Mary paused for a moment, "Adults are complicated. Hey Georgie, could you throw me my camping stuff?"

George left the window for a moment before running back with a duffel bag roughly twice his size. He awkwardly flipped the bag out of the window. "Why do you need this? Can I come with you?"

"Mom's pretty mad so I've got to go for a bit. I'll come home soon though, okay?"

"You promise?"

"I promise."

George hung out of the window with his pinky finger extended. Mary stood on her tippy toes and reached as far as she could. She managed to grab her brother's hand and accepted his pinky swear.

"Wait!" George hurried away from the window. He returned moments later with his stuffed bear, which he dropped down to Mary. "Take Mister Purdy with you. He will keep you safe."

Chapter Seven

After being kicked out of the house, Mary once again found herself hiding out in the forest. The intimidatingly deep, dark forest was much more welcoming in the day. The branches that only twelve hours ago resembled dismembered arms reaching out from the shadows now only looked like, well, tree limbs. In fact, during daylight hours, the forest was actually quite pleasant. Mary could see where she was walking, and knew that the creatures that went bump in the night were only squirrels and songbirds. Although, if she did happen upon a chupacabra or sasquatch, Mary was confident she'd think of an escape plan.

Mary dropped the extremely heavy camping bag that had begun to cut into her shoulder, and hurried towards the creek which ran through the middle of the forest. Crouching over the small stream, Mary splashed water on herself and did her best to wash away all the remaining slime. The freezing cold water in the creek stung her face; she wasn't aware that she had gotten sun-burnt while out hunting with Friedrich. Once she was as cleaned up as she was going to be, she took a few minutes to take in her surroundings. The trees were thick enough to provide cover, but also sparse enough in spots to let in a few rays of sun. There was a nearby saskatoon berry bush, and a few patches of wild strawberries. And the best part, there were no adults or bullies for miles. Other than the temperature of the water, this was going to be a perfect place for Mary to set-up camp. She also really didn't want to carry the camping supplies any further if it could be helped.

Mary reached into the bag and pulled out a spool of rope and a small tarp. She pushed against two spindly nearby trees to test their strength. After shaking and kicking them and doing all she could to mimic a wind storm, Mary was satisfied with the spot that she picked, and used the rope to hang the tarp between the two trees. She was going to be quite comfortable here, unless it snowed. Mary knew that was extremely unlikely to happen in June, but she always liked to be prepared.

Once the tarp was strung up, Mary made a clearing underneath. She brushed away the twigs and pine needles, revealing a smooth dusty patch. She retrieved a small wool blanket from the camping bag, which she laid out underneath the tarp. It was almost perfect, but something was still missing. Mary felt around, checking out the contents of the bag. *What else is in here,* she wondered. A fishing rod, and some hooks. *Ouch!* A mug. A coffee percolator... Eventually she pulled out George's teddy bear, Mr. Purdy. She placed the scruffy old teddy bear on the blanket and smiled.

Mary sat down next to the bear and stared out at the creek. For what felt like the first time in her short life, she finally had a moment of peace. She took the slightly gooey book out of her book bag and began to read. After only a few pages though, the hairs on the back of Mary's neck stood up as she began to sense that something was watching her...

A breathy moan was coming from behind the saskatoon berry bush.

Arrrroooooaaaggghhhh...

Mary froze. *Was it a bear? A cougar? A pervert?* Mary's Mom had warned her about all three, but she was never told what to do if she was confronted by one. Never one to run away from danger, Mary retrieved a small pocket knife from a pouch in the camping bag. It took Mary a moment to remember that she had something so much better than a small knife. She tossed the scuffed up old Swiss Army knife aside and grabbed the ray gun.

Holding the ray gun in front of her, like she saw a cop do in a movie once, Mary carefully crept towards the groaning shrubbery, and used her foot to kick away part of the bush revealing what was making the sound. Expecting a wild animal, Mary couldn't believe her eyes when she came face to face with what appeared to be... an alien. It was lanky and grey, with hints of blue scales. Or was that its suit? Anyone else would have been terrified, but Mary recognized the pain in the alien's giant brown eyes. They reminded her of a cow's eyes, gentle.

"Hello," Mary spoke softly.

The alien continued to breathe deeply, in pain. Mary could tell that it wasn't a threat.

"I'm Mary... What is your name?"

The wounded alien looked up at her. Its breathing slowed. "I'm not going to hurt you." As Mary spoke those words, she sensed that didn't need to say them out loud; the alien understood her somehow.

Mary looked around and found a thick branch which must have blown down in the last big windstorm. Spotting the pocket knife she cast aside moments before, she picked it up and opened the blade, causing the alien to wince slightly.

"It's okay," Mary said softly, never taking her eyes off the alien, making sure it was watching as she started to scrape some off some of the rough bark. She put the knife away, and offered the branch to the alien. "Here, it's to help you walk."

Mary reached towards the alien and tried to help it stand up. It was only then that she realized the extent of its injuries. Its leg was bleeding, but its most severe injury was its missing hand. Mary couldn't help but notice that the alien had red blood. The men performing the radio shows always talked about little green men from Mars. She never would have expected an alien to have the same fluids as a human.

Realizing that the first aid kit in her camping bag was out of band aids and gauze, thanks to a mysterious hunting incident with Friedrich weeks prior that she knew little about, Mary ripped the sleeves off her plaid printed button up shirt. The sleeves were still wet from earlier, but they would be better than nothing. She had worn a long-sleeved shirt out hunting so that she wouldn't get sun burnt while out with Friedrich, completely forgetting that her face was exposed. She imaged that by now, she probably looked like a tomato.

Mary slowly reached towards the alien's wounded arm. "Could I see your arm please? We need to stop the bleeding."

Mary gently, but tightly, made a tourniquet out of her shirt sleeves. She wrapped the first one around the alien's wrist and the second one around its injured shin. The alien let out a series of odd clicking noises and gestured towards the quarry. Through their innate shared understanding of one another, Mary helped the alien to stand up and led it to the gravel quarry where she had found the space ship wreckage the night before.

After slowly making their way through the forest, Mary and the alien found themselves at the edge of the quarry embankment. All the wreckage was gone, as if nothing had ever happened. Mary and the alien looked to one another, knowingly. "It's okay, you can stay with me."

Hand in hand, Mary and the alien walked back into the forest.

Chapter Eight

Mary kneeled next to the alien, who was sitting by the stream at Mary's encampment. Its long thin legs stretched out in front of it, the alien was at least seven feet tall with a surprisingly short torso. Mary had the contents of her first aid kit spread out along the rocks. It contained a small pair of scissors, a scalpel, material to craft a splint, cotton balls, iodine, and even several ration packets. She used to think it was weird that her late stepfather would shop at military surplus stores, but now she was happy that he had. Other than its lack of bandaging, the kit had nearly everything one might need if they came across someone injured in the woods. Even if that person was from outer space.

"Let me see your arm," Mary said while gesturing to the alien's wounded stump. The alien cautiously extended its arm as Mary slowly poured a cup of water over the alien's injury.

"We need to clean it out."

The alien let out a series of clicks, indicating that it was in pain.

"I'm so sorry. It's going to get worse," Mary said as she retrieved a bottle of iodine from the kit, before gently dabbing it on the alien's wound with a cotton ball.

CLICK CLICK CLICK CLICK...

Chapter Nine

Sunday, June 15th

The sun was beaming through the windows of the Schmidt family's single floor rancher. The light refracted off the little bits of dust that were lazily floating in the air. Some of Margaret's busybody friends had made comments about the state of the house, but they just didn't understand that dust was natural, and that's just what happened when you had kids running in and out of the house all day and you lived next to a farmyard. At least that's what Margaret told herself.

It was the early afternoon, and Margaret was resting with her feet up. With her abusive husband recently vaporized, and her uppity daughter ousted to the forest, this was the first time in years that she was able to lay back and relax with a magazine. *Sure, I'm probably going to have nightmares about this ordeal for the rest of my life, but who doesn't have issues,* Margaret rationalized. The ever-present George was usually annoying, but had seemed to have gotten the hint that he should be quiet and focus on his colouring books that day. Margaret needed some me time.

Margaret closed the previous month's edition of Chatelaine on her chest and without looking, picked up the glass of lemonade that she had sitting on the floor. She had considered spicing up the drink and adding some liquor to it, but she personally wasn't much of a drinker. After being married to that drunk Friedrich, for three – nearly four years – the smell of alcohol made her sick. Her first husband Douglas wasn't much of a drinker either, which is why his liver cancer diagnosis had been so shocking.

Margaret took a long sip of the tart lemonade and placed the drink on the floor, then reopened the magazine and continued to read. She didn't much care for Chatelaine as she thought it was too feminine, but there weren't many other options for sale at the local general store. No sooner than Margaret started the next article, than there was a knock at the door.

"Can you go get that for Mama, Georgie?"

Annoying or not, sometimes it was helpful to have a small butler. Not to be a pessimist, but Margaret knew she would never be wealthy. Especially since she left most of her belongings back in Ukraine when she migrated here. Not wanting her own kids to go through the struggles of learning a second language, she never spoke her mother tongue at home. She rationalised that most children weren't smart enough to learn more than one language anyway. It had been so difficult to start a new life alone when she was just fifteen, that now that she was grown, it was fun for her to pretend that she had a little servant. Little Georgie hopped up from the carpeted floor, accidentally spilling his box of pencil crayons in the process. "Yes, Mama."

Margaret was proud of how obedient her son was; she didn't know that he only listened because he was afraid of being kicked out of the house like his older sister. George hastily ran to the front of the house and opened the screen door for the two stately looking men that were on the other side.

"Why, hello there little guy! Is your daddy home?" Constable Stone, a stocky middle-aged man, asked.

"My dad is dead. He died a long time ago," George responded sadly, holding back tears. He didn't understand why a stranger would show up only to ask him something so mean. Not only that, but the constable's large mustache made him uncomfortable. It reminded him of something that their old cat used to leave on the front step.

"Oh. I'm sorry little fella…" Constable Stone turned to his partner, "Maybe this is the wrong house?"

The second agent, District Game Warden Smith, a clean cut and much more strong jawed man than his partner, crouched down in front of George.

"We're asking about this man," Warden Smith asked, flashing George a photo of Friedrich.

"Oh! You mean Bad Daddy. He isn't home right now," George said as he choked back tears.

Margaret abruptly stepped in front of George. To the officers, it might have appeared that she was protecting her son, but she really just wanted her toddler son to stop blathering.

Their family was already the talk of the town; Margaret didn't want everyone to know that her daughter was also a killer. "Why hello officers. What seems to be the problem?"

"Hello, ma'am. We are looking for your husband. Friedrich Johnson," Warden Smith said while standing up. His knees cracked, and he resented having to bend down to talk to a child in the first place.

"Can I ask why?" Margaret asked hesitantly.

"We have reports that he has been participating in some extremely *illicit* activity," Constable Stone spoke under a hushed breath. The word illicit caused the constable's moustache to flare out ever so slightly.

"What has he done this time?" Margaret could feel the hair on the back of her neck begin to prickle.

"He was reported for killing innocent—"

"Poaching, ma'am. Your husband is a poacher," Warden Smith bluntly announced before his partner could continue.

"Poaching? Whew. I thought you were gonna say that he hurt someone," Margaret rubbed her arms in nervous relief.

"Poaching *is* serious. That's why the Game Department was established," Warden Smith scolded.

"Yeah, if your husband had robbed a bank or caused bodily harm to a person, then the BCPP would be here right now—" Constable Stone rambled on.

"Where is your husband?" his boss, Warden Smith, interrupted.

Warden Smith knew that he cast a much more imposing figure than his subordinate and was not afraid to embrace it.

"Maybe this is all a misunderstanding that he can clear up?" Constable Stone offered sympathetically to Margaret, while giving his superior officer a sideways glance.

Wow, they must've practiced this "Mutt and Jeff" routine, Margaret thought to herself. She looked down at the rusty old stain on the floor right by the door, left behind from Friedrich's constantly leaking hunting bag.

"Oh, no. It's not a misunderstanding. He definitely did it," Margaret finally spoke.

"Sh-shooting on protected lands?" Constable Stone sputtered, taken back by Margaret's nonchalant attitude.

"Oh yeah."

"Raiding the neighbours hen house?" Warden Smith asked with a raised eyebrow.

"Sounds like Friedrich."

"Did he also shoot that poor gorilla at the zoo?" Constable Stone asked, his moustache continuing to sway with each word.

"That one, probably not."

"Your husband sounds like a real piece of work, ma'am. Where is he?" Warden Smith asked, while opening a small black notebook.

"I'd turn him in in a heartbeat, but I haven't seen him in two days."

"Why not?" Warned Smith asked with a raised eyebrow. He couldn't imagine a husband not coming home to his wife every night. Unless the husband was a good for nothing debaucher.

That is a good question. Margaret paused for a moment, thinking up a believable backstory. What would be believable, but also not cause the townspeople to think any worse of her… "I heard a rumour he took off with that gal down at the corner store. He was always philandering. For all his faults, Friedrich was—is—still quite a charmer."

Warden Smith looked at the picture of Friedrich that he had shown George moments ago, with a raised eyebrow. Based off his appearance, Warden Smith wouldn't have described Friedrich as a charmer. *Maybe Constable Stone was right, maybe I do judge people too quickly.* Realizing he was getting distracted, Smith fixed his posture and cleared his throat, "Mind if we take a look inside?"

"I'd tell you if he was here," Margaret said, as kindly as she could without being defensive. She perfected this tone in her last relationship.

"We just need to be certain." Warden Smith stepped past Margaret, and into the house. Constable Stone followed his boss, while mouthing the words *I am so sorry* to Margaret.

Warden Smith and Constable Stone were both taken back by the situation in the Schmidt house. Large stacks of newspapers were piled up on a dinner tray. The lone house plant had clearly been used as an ashtray. Several stray beer tins were sitting in the corner of the room. And in the center of it all, little George was sprawled out across the thick green carpeting, colouring. The officers looked to each other knowingly, as if they were making a secret pact to each other to never complain about how clean their wives kept their own houses ever again.

"What does your husband do for a living, Miss—"

"It's Margaret," Margaret interrupted Constable Stone. "Anyway, he doesn't do much. Hunting mostly. Or poaching, as you gentlemen are now calling it."

Warden Smith crouched down next to George stiffly. "Who's that in the picture, son?"

"You're not great with kids, are you, boss?" Constable Stone asked, turning away from Margaret to address his boss.

"This is me. This is my mom. This is my sister, Mary. And this is Bad Daddy as a pile of goo!" George explained, excitedly.

"Kids are so creative—" Margaret justified.

"And where is your sister at right now?" Warden Smith said, interrupting Margaret. "Can we talk to her?"

"Oh, no. Mary's gone now. Mommy made her leave." George's enthusiasm faded as he remembered that Mary was no longer at home. He looked back at his paper, and returned to drawing.

"Your mother kicked out your sister?" Constable Stone asked with concern,

Sensing that things were going south, Margaret once again stepped between George and the officers. "It feels like you're asking a lot of questions! Why don't you come back later? I'll bake a pie. Lemon curd? Do you like lemon—"

Ignoring Margaret, Warden Smith continued to try to speak with George. "Why don't you tell me about your sister?

"Her name is Mary. She's my big sister, and I love her very much. Mommy doesn't though, so she made Mary live in the forest."

"Like you said, kids are so creative?" Constable Stone offered to Margaret.

"No, he's right. Mary is such a little survivalist, trying to be like Jacque Cousteau, or James Cook...? One of those people that school shoved down her throat. So, she went out camping. She'll be home later."

The officers looked at each other, and then to Margaret. "Well, that sounds fine to me. After all, we're here on

poaching charges. Not anything about your children," Warden Smith said with a shrug.

"As long as you make sure she is home tonight, it should be fine, I guess... Please telephone us when Friedrich comes home though," Constable Stone asked, while following Warden Smith out of the house.

Margaret followed the officers and locked the door behind them. She returned to the living room, where she shot George an angry glare.

"Did I do something wrong?"

"Go back to colouring." Margaret laid back down on the couch. She had lost her place in the magazine. Frustrated, she leaned over and picked up her glass of lemonade which had gotten warm.

"Can I go visit Mary?" George said while putting his art supplies away.

Margaret could feel the vein in the side of her head start to throb. She closed her eyes and did her best to imagine that she was on a beach somewhere tropical and far away.

Chapter Ten

Most kids that had been kicked out of their homes would panic and plead for their parents' forgiveness. Not Mary though. While her mother dealt with the conservation officers and chores back home, Mary was in her element. She had her fishing gear, a new friend, and her radio. What more did a kid need?

From dawn until dusk, Mary worked to teach the alien outdoor skills. She didn't know how long that they would be out here together for and thought that she might as well teach the alien everything that she knew about surviving in the woods. What if the alien had forests back home and got lost again one day? Mary wanted it to be prepared. Although she would never admit it out loud, Mary had learned a few useful things from Friedrich over the years, and now that he was dead it felt like she should share some of that knowledge.

The two of them went fishing, fastened spears, and exchanged stories of each of their life's adventures. Mary still wasn't quite sure how she understood the alien; she had heard about this sort of communication before, in a radio show about gypsies and psychics, but word escaped her. Cards on the table though, if Mary had to pick one favourite moment from the day, it was when the two of them were sitting together at the camp enjoying the music from the radio.

Night was going to be there soon, and it was starting to get cold. Even though Falkland was in the middle of a semi-arid desert and got quite hot during the summer months, it could become chilly at night. Unbeknownst to her, the ray gun had a mode which made it shoot an electrical beam rather than turning its target gelatinous. The alien showed her this feature and used it to start a small fire when it became obvious that the one-handed alien was never going to be able to start a fire by rubbing two twigs together.

By dark, the two friends had worked up quite an appetite. They had tried hunting for rabbit, but it didn't go well as this was before the alien taught Mary about the ray gun's electrical mode. Thankfully they managed to catch several trout, as the accidental batch of rabbit Jell-O was nauseating. Mary sliced the fish open and skewered them on two green branches. The branches needed to be fresh, otherwise they would catch fire and ruin dinner. Mary had also soaked them in the water before hand, just to be safe. Once the fish scales began to turn crispy and peel off of the fish, Mary took them off of the fire.

"I'm sorry. I didn't pack any dishes," Mary spoke softly as she passed a trout to the alien.

Although she had never seen the alien open its mouth, Mary assumed that it at least had one. It took her by surprise though to see the alien's small facial slit stretch open widely enough to fit the entire fish in its mouth and swallow it whole.

Mary was thankful it was dark out, because seeing the alien's surprisingly toothy mouth in all the detail of daylight might have finally scared her.

Sensing Mary's discomfort, the alien opened its mouth again, reached down its throat, and pulled out the still-intact fish skeleton and carefully offered it back to Mary. It clearly didn't want to come across as rude.

After dinner, Mary bathed in the frigid creek. The one thing she didn't have in her bag was a tooth brush, so Mary had used her finger and some berries for flavour. It didn't work as well as she had hoped, and now she had seeds stuck in her teeth. After splashing around in the chilly water, Mary cozied up with the alien next to the fire. There was a clearing in the trees just above the camp which allowed the sky to show through. The night sky was strewn with stars, as if a handful of glitter had gotten stuck in the sky. Mary looked at the alien in wonder. "Which star did you come from?"

The alien looked up to the sky. It sat in thought for a moment, before pointing to a star in the Orion Constellation.

"Your home is in that cluster?"

The alien drew a circle in the air and moved its hand through it.

"A planet that moves through it?" Mary paused for a moment, thinking carefully about her next question.

"I don't want to seem dumb, but I've got to know. What is the difference between a star and a planet? We haven't gotten that far in school yet."

The alien let out a series of quiet clicking sounds. Mary nodded, knowingly. The two continued to stare off into the stars letting the world around them disappear.

"When your friends come back, I hope I can go with you." The alien carefully wrapped its good arm around Mary. She tried to rest her head on its shoulder but was only able to reach its elbow. Either way, this was the most comfortable she had ever felt. Although Mary knew that no one would believe her if she told them about the alien's home world, she took pride in being the only person on Earth to know something so special.

Chapter Eleven

Friday, June 20th

Susan Webb stood in front of her less-than-interested third grade class. She understood that children that age didn't always have the longest attention spans, but she still wished that they would at least pretend to listen to her more. Even though the class only had ten students in it, they could get quite rambunctious. Being disrespected was probably one of Susan's biggest pet peeves, but she resigned herself to the fact that was just life. Besides, these children couldn't help it; some of them had terrible parents. Or rather, most did. But Susan would never share that thought out loud.

Her late-ex-fiancé Douglas and she had been planning on having children, but their life together didn't turn out as planned. They were high school sweethearts who had moved to Falkland in 1937, shortly before the second World War began. As an Engineering Officer with the United States Army, Douglas was privy to news about global events before the general public. Sensing that international troubles were brewing, and knowing that army desertion was a capital offence,

Douglas had convinced Susan to start over in Falkland with him. All they had to do was change their last names. However, once they arrived in Falkland, Douglas was quickly entranced by one of the local harlots. Susan knew the only reason he would ever betray her is if he just couldn't help it. Deep down she knew that he loved her...

Because of that unmet maternal longing, Susan was passionate about imparting as much knowledge as she could onto her students. At least today's science class subject was outer space. That, and dinosaurs, always got the most interest. It also gave her an excuse to wear her fantastic planet patterned dress that she sewed for herself last summer. Back in Tacoma, Susan had planned on becoming a seamstress.

"So, thanks to Sir Isaac Newton's discovery in 1687, we understand that our moon actually controls the tides of the ocean. How interesting is that?" Susan exclaimed perhaps a little too excitedly. She cleared her throat, realizing that her voice was coming across as more perturbed than necessary. "Does anyone have any questions so far?"

"What is the difference between stars and planets?" Mary asked, only raising her arm half way in an attempt to shield her increasingly tattered shirt.

While she preferred when students waited until they were called on directly to ask a question, Susan was happy to see that Mary Schmidt was participating. Although Mary was one of Susan Webb's best students, there were days when she seemed distracted or afraid to speak up. It gave Susan hope each time that Mary would assert herself. That child would always have a soft spot in Susan's heart. If Douglas hadn't been so overcome with lust for that awful Margaret woman, Mary might have wound up in Susan's womb. She was worried at how scruffy Mary looked today though; it was as if she had been rolling around in dirt all week. "That's a great question, Mary. Stars produce their own light because of radiation, and planets orbit around them. Planets also don't produce their own light."

Mary smiled, happy to know that the alien was right and that she hadn't misunderstood it. Unable to allow her to have this lone moment of reprieve, the class bullies decided that now was the time to start mocking Mary. It was as though they shared their own psychic connection.

"Planets orbit stars the way gross men orbit Mary's Mom!" Don yelled out. Not content with merely tripping Mary down the school steps, he had to take her down in class too.

"Don, go to the principal's office," Susan sighed.

The rest of the class chuckled, causing Don to blush. The chubby bully stood up. His increasingly pink baby-like face betraying the tough guy image he tried to present. "Worth it," Don muttered, as he left the class.

Susan looked at the class with as stern a glare as she could muster. She wished she looked more authoritative, but resigned herself to the fact that she just wasn't that kind of person. "Moving on… The ninth planet in our solar system is Pluto. This little planet was discovered very recently actually. In 1930! Some of your parents were probably sitting in these very same desks when the discovery was made."

"Mary's parents didn't even go to school," Lucy, the curly blonde-haired preacher's daughter and passionate tormentor of Mary, snarked.

"Do you want to go to the office too, Lucy?"

"What is past Pluto?" a shy student from the back of the class asked.

"Nothing that we know of, yet. Pluto was only discovered seventeen years ago though, so just think what else could be out there!" Susan exclaimed with a restrained excitement; she really did love to teach about space.

Mary raised her hand. Her earlier confidence staring to fade.

"Yes Mary?"

"I, um, heard that there is a tenth planet." "Where did you hear that?"

"Just, from a friend."

"Mary, we all know you don't have friends," Lucy called out.

"Lucy, go sit in the hall."

Lucy shot Mary a smirk as she walked out of the classroom. Because of the rule of threes, the third bully, Ricky, the one that looked like his hair was slicked with motor oil, used this time to make a kissy face at Mary. She knew that it meant she was a butt kisser – there was no way that either of those two gross boys would ever flirt with her.

Noticing that it was almost three o'clock, Susan decided that she should end this class. Besides, as much as she loved space, the brats in this class were starting to get exhausting. "That's all for today though, class," Susan called out, "Don't forget that your dioramas are due next week. This is your last project of the year, so it's extra important!"

With her head down, Mary nearly snuck out of the classroom unnoticed. Susan managed to catch her just in time.

"Mary, could I talk with you?"

"What is the problem, Miss Webb?" There was a weariness to Mary's eyes that made her teacher even more concerned than normal.

To Susan it looked as if Mary had been sleeping rough. "There's no problem. I am just wondering how you are. How things are with you and your Mom?"

"Oh, you know…" Mary looked down at her feet, hesitant to reveal too much. She noticed how dirty her shoes were, and started kicking little bits of clay off, onto the wooden classroom floor.

"You're not in trouble. I promise. I am just worried because you are turning into a little," Susan searched for the right word, "A little bit of a ragamuffin, and I want to make sure that things are okay at home. I understand that sometimes your parents, um, get distracted from their parenting duties."

"It's fine," Mary insisted. "I've been staying with a friend."

"Is that the friend that told you about the planet past Pluto?"

Mary didn't respond. She continued to kick off flecks of dirt from her sneakers.

"How do you know this person, Mary?"

"I need to go, Miss Webb. Thank you for looking out for me. I'm fine though. Promise." Mary turned and hurried away, leaving Susan Webb even more concerned than she already was.

Chapter Twelve

It was a Saturday morning just like every other Saturday morning for the Bishop family. The three of them were gathered around their over sized oak dining room table for their weekly family breakfast. In front of each family member was a similarly laid out plate of slightly burnt bacon, sunny side up eggs, and apple butter toast. The entire house had a slight maple scent from the syrup that the family matriarch, Helen, would add to the bacon. Some people might have called this breakfast excessive. For the Bishops however, this was routine. All little Lucy Bishop really wanted to eat though was a damned bowl of cereal.

Be present at our table, Lord.

Be here and everywhere adored.

Thy people bless, and grant that we, may feast in paradise with thee.

Lucy's father, Raymond Bishop, the town's preacher, always insisted on saying this prayer before breakfast. Sometimes they would forget to do it before their nightly dinners, but Helen and Raymond insisted that Saturday morning family break- fast was treated with the utmost importance. Since Raymond worked Sundays and left the house early during the week, it was the one day that they had free to spend together as a family. Lucy often ate dinners alone, or in the kitchen with her mother. She didn't understand the importance of seeing her father on Saturdays and was apathetic about the entire ritual.

Raymond wasn't always a man of God. In fact, he used to be a real estate agent in the nearby town of Vernon. He wasn't the most reputable realtor in the region though, and he had burned a lot of bridges. Not necessarily because Raymond was a bad person; he was only trying to get ahead the best that he knew how. When the Great Depression hit, Raymond and his wife, Helen, took this as an opportunity to get out of Dodge and moved to Falkland. The town was just starting to grow and felt like the perfect place for a fresh start. No one knew them yet, and there were very few people for them to get to know. Life would be easy.

Raymond had decided to become a preacher once he learned that Protestant preachers did not need to be ordained, unlike their pastoral counterparts. Most of the townspeople didn't realize that though, and because he was such a char-ismatic man, he quickly settled into his new role. Lucy was born nearly five years after the Bishop's moved to Falkland, although it wasn't for their lack of trying... Her parents were so proud of their precocious little girl. She was their greatest prize. Their little golden child. Her blonde curls were identical to her mothers, while she shared her father's blue eyes.

When Lucy grew older, she would grow to think that Helen and Raymond felt comfortable talking with her as an adult because of everything they projected on her. To them though, they simply wanted her to know how much she was loved, even though Lucy found their prayers and old person stories to be incredibly dull.

Lucy picked at her breakfast, as she did every Saturday: a few bites of bacon here, a few bites of toast there. Her mother would throw the rest of it in the garbage shortly after Lucy slid her plate to the center of the table and left the house to go and find either Don or Ricky. Neither of them ever had weekend family events to attend. Lucy liked that about them.

Chapter Thirteen

While the Bishop family had their Saturday breakfast, and Mary was up to who knows what, Margaret was sunbathing in the front lawn. Growing sick of the dust in the house, Margaret had been spending more and more time outside in the sun. It was so refreshing to not have a family to take care of. Yes, George was still around, but he mostly kept to himself. At this moment, he was teaching himself how to do flips on the rusty old tire swing. As long as he stayed quiet, Margaret was content. Except for the persistent hum of insects in the tall dry grass, life was silent. Stretched out so far that she only her upper torso remained in the lawn chair, Margaret let out a huge sigh. *This is the life.*

Just as Margaret was about to doze off, she was startled by a loud ding ding ding! She shot up out of her seat, and spotted Susan Webb, Mary's teacher and Margaret's nemesis biking towards her. *Ugh, of course she would put a bell on her bicycle,* Margaret thought to herself. Susan was so clingy. So hopelessly needy. In Ukraine, they called women like Susan коза –

roughly translated to "annoying goat" – but Margaret would never speak her first language here. It was safer this way.

Margaret's first husband, the father of her children and the real love of her life, Douglas had moved to Falkland to escape from Susan. She knew that Susan and Douglas were high school sweethearts, but as he told her, their relationship had soured as the years went on. He told Susan that he had to move to Canada, to escape the war. An impending war was a silly excuse he made up to escape her; Douglas didn't think that one would actually take place. He told Margaret how guilty he felt, as if he had willed this into being, while reading about the rise of Hitler in the newspaper. At the time Douglas was just a silly boy who wanted to be free from his girlfriend – he never thought Susan would follow him all of the way to Falkland, but when he arrived in town, she was already here! Not only had she pursued him all of the way from the United States into Canada, but she had somehow managed to arrive there before him. The woman was relentless.

"Marg! Hi! I hope I'm not disturbing you..." Susan trailed off as she dismounted from her bicycle. The bike was blue and matched perfectly with her gingham print sun dress. Susan was always dressed for the occasion, no matter what that occasion may be. Margaret liked to joke that Susan would dress up for the opening of an envelope.

"Susan Webb... I haven't seen you in ages." Margaret scoffed, while standing up.

"You'd see more of me if you came to Mary's parent teacher meetings," Susan replied in a saccharine sweet tone that Margaret detested.

"What do you want? What did Mary do this time?" Margaret eyed Susan up and down. She figured that she could beat her in a fistfight, if she had to.

"Mary hasn't done anything. Is she here though? I'd love to say hi," Susan said as she peered around the yard.

"No. She's out camping." Margaret really disliked how close Susan tried to be with Mary. It made her deeply uncomfortable.

Susan continued to look around at the Schmidt property. She knew Margaret had a difficult life, having only migrated to Canada in the 1930s, but thought that Margaret should work harder to keep a tidy house. After all, as Susan always said, a clean home is the mark of a clean mind. She would never understand what attracted so many men, including Susan's former fiancé, to this woman. "Camping just for the weekend, or something more permanent?"

"Who knows. Children these days do what they want." Margaret didn't like what Susan was insinuating, even if it was true. She knew that she wasn't the perfect parent but didn't need it to be rubbed in her face every waking moment of the day.

"Okay, I'll cut to the chase. I'm here because Mary looks like she hasn't been bathing lately, and I just wanted to make sure that she is being taken care of."

Margaret shrugged, "Kids get dirty outside."

George walked up behind Margaret and gave her leg a big hug. Susan crouched down to George's eye level, which was also level to Margaret's knee. "Hi Georgie. Do you remember when you last saw your sister?"

"Seven days ago. I know, because I count. Mom, can I have a snack?" George asked, changing his focus from Susan Webb to his mother.

"Why are you asking me? You know where to find them," Margaret shook George off her leg and shooed him away. She momentarily debated kneeing Susan in the face but thought better of it.

"A week feels like a long time for a little girl to be out camping with friends."

"Friends? Pfff, my Mary doesn't have friends. She's out there alone. She's tough, like her mom."

"No one has ever suggested otherwise, Margaret."

"I know not everyone likes me. Some women get envious that I can land a man so easily," Margaret replied defensively.

"You slept with my fiancé," Susan spoke bluntly. There it was, that horrible thing that Susan always tried to forget about and yet somehow thought about every single day.

"Oh, that's right, Douglas was with you first. I always forget. He was such an honorable man though, to marry me when I fell pregnant with Mary."

"You didn't deserve Douglas, and you certainly don't deserve a daughter as bright as Mary," Susan rebutted.

Although the two women were speaking outside, the atmosphere felt as tense as an elastic band that was ready to snap.

By now, both Margaret and Susan were standing toe to toe. The contrast between them was striking. Susan was smiley, blonde, and slight, while Margaret had dark, nearly black hair, broad shoulders, and a permanently tired look on her face. While nearly the exact same age, to onlookers it would have been quite clear to which one of them had seemingly lived multiple lives.

Margaret broke the tension with a laugh. She honestly couldn't remember the last time she made that sound. Her sharp-yet-sarcastic chuckle caused the metaphorical elastic band of tension to snap and hit Susan in the face. Susan backed up, appalled. "Sounds like envy to me, Susan. Is that all? Is there anything else you want to talk about?" Margaret barked, unwavering in her stance.

"Mary needs to show up to class clean on Monday, or else I am reporting you to the authorities." Susan indignantly said as she awkwardly hopped back on her blue bicycle and rode away.

Margaret watched until Susan was completely out of sight, before she crumbled onto the dusty ground. She wasn't going to cry, because only the weak let the opinions of others bother them; she was just so deeply exhausted. After several minutes, Margaret got up and started walking back to the house, when she spotted two recognisable small figures way out in the farmer's field behind the house.

"George! Get your butt back here!" Margaret hollered out to her son, who had wandered off a bit further than was acceptable for a toddler.

"Just a minute, mama!" George yelled back as politely as he could, not wanting to upset his mother even more.

Mary waded through the tall dry grass in the farmer's field and gave her little brother a big hug. "I've missed you so much."

George passed his sister a paper bag full of food. He had grabbed from the kitchen while his mom was talking with that lady in the front yard.

"I missed you too, Mary. Mom is mean now. I thought she would be nice now that Bad Daddy is gone, but…" George trailed off. "She's much worse."

"I'm sorry, Georgie."

"When are you coming home?"

"I don't know exactly. I made a friend, but they need my help."

"Mary! Get over here now!" Margaret shrieked as she grew closer and closer.

"I should go," Mary said as she hugged her brother tightly before turning and running away.

"Lord help me, Mary! You can't live in the woods forever!" Margaret yelled.

Mary quickly made her way across the field, before disappearing into the woods.

"At least wash your face!"

As soon as he was certain Mary was safely away from their mother, George turned to walk back home. Unknowingly, he walked through the exact spot that his stepfather was gelatinized a short week before. There were no signs of Friedrich left, save for a few fat buzzing flies.

Chapter Fourteen

Winded from her mad dash across of her family's yard and the connecting farmer's field, Mary was huffing and puffing by the time she returned to the forest. She had never run that fast before and was impressed with herself. It was a good thing that the weather was changing and clouds were rolling in, as Mary needed a break from the heat. Even though the sweat from her forehead was running into her eyes and burning something fierce, Mary was in a great mood and was looking forward to sharing her haul of snacks – mostly bread and apples – with the alien. *Do aliens like apples?* When she reached the camp though, her excitement quickly diminished.

The alien was leaning lethargically against one of the pine trees. The blue hue of its scales had faded away, leaving its skin entirely grey and slightly translucent. The alien's all too human circulatory system was visible, just under its increasingly thin grey skin. A thin milky coating was beginning to cover the alien's giant bovine-esque eyes.

"You don't look so good," Mary offered sympathetically as she crouched down next to the alien. "Here, eat this," Mary said as she passed the alien an apple.

She placed her hand on the alien's large forehead, which was cold to the touch. Mary didn't know much, or anything really, about the health of aliens, but she could tell that something was very wrong. She prayed that there was some truth to the adage about an apple a day keeping doctors away.

Maybe some rosehip tea would help? They weren't supposed to be in season yet, but Mary swore she spotted some growing along the perimeter of the forest during her run. She grabbed the bucket made of birch bark that she had made a few days earlier and walked down to the edge of the creek to retrieve some water.

While filling up the bucket, Mary caught a glimpse of her reflection in the water. Never a vain child, Mary was still taken back by how dirty her face was. She looked like a hobo! Mary frantically splashed water on her face, determined to look more like the spry nine-year-old she remembered seeing in her bedroom mirror only a week ago. Unaware of just how bad this day was going to get, Mary was startled when she spotted her rivals Lucy and Ricky making their way up the creek.

"Oh no..." Mary hurried back to the alien. "You need to hide. Now!" The alien looked at Mary sluggishly.

"Some bad kids are coming! They can't know about you!" Mary exclaimed as loudly as she could without yelling. She tried desperately to coerce the alien away from the tree that it was leaning on and into the bushes. Still about twenty yards away from Mary's camp, Lucy and Ricky were hopping from rock to rock, slowly making their way up the creek.

"It was so rude of Don to ditch us! The tree house ladder is a two-man job!" Lucy whined.

"Yeah, stupid Don..." Ricky muttered. He felt bad about insulting his friend when he wasn't around.

"You're just going to have to pull me up the ladder yourself." "Not a problem, Luc. I'm stronger than Don, anyway,"

Ricky proclaimed, flexing his undeveloped arm muscles.

Lucy rolled her eyes and continued jumping between the stones. When she looked up again, Lucy noticed Mary frantically pacing around by a tree. *Was she talking to herself?* "Wait, is that Mary up ahead?"

"The little sheep girl?" Ricky offered.

Noticing that Lucy and Ricky had made their way to the camp, Mary stood nervously in front of the bushes that the alien was hiding in.

"Hi Maryyyyy..." Lucy mocked.

"Ba ba black sheep," Ricky reciprocated with a giggle.

"Hi you two. What are you doing here?" Mary said while shifting her weight from foot to foot.

"More like, what are you doing here?" Lucy asked while looking at Mary's camp judgingly.

Ricky paced around, picking up and examining Mary's belongings. He looked at the teddy bear, Mr. Purdy, and laughed. I think she lives here, Luc."

"You're even poorer than I thought!" Lucy joined in with Ricky's laughter.

"Just leave me alone," Mary spoke meekly, not wanting to further provoke the bullies. She walked towards them slowly, in an attempt to guide them away from her camp.

"But mocking you is just so much fun!" Lucy cooed.

"You fish, Mary?" Ricky asked, while examining Mary's taped up old fishing rod.

"Give that back!" Mary yelled, lunging at Ricky trying to get her hands on her prized possession.

"Did your family run out of pet sheep to eat?" Lucy continued to mock.

"Maybe she's Catholic now?" Ricky suggested while holding the fishing rod just out of Mary's reach.

"That doesn't even make sense, Ricky," Lucy snapped.

"My grandparents only eat fish on Fridays. It's a religious thing—" Ricky tried to explain.

"No one cares," Lucy barked while grabbing the fishing rod from Ricky and snapping it in half.

Mary's heart went into her stomach. She didn't have any more duck tape to repair the rod. "Why would you do that? Why do you hate me so much for having less than you?"

Just as hot tears began to fill Mary's eyes, the alien leapt out of the bushes!

"B-behind y-you," Ricky stammered.

Lucy could only manage to let out a tiny scream.

The alien leaned over top of Mary. Her small stature only emphasized its terrifying seven-foot frame. It opened its mouth and stretched its jaw so widely that it looked as if it was going to eat one of the children's heads, and let out a few slight clicks before unleashing a deafening high pitch scream.

Click, click... EEEEEEEEEEEEEE!

Ricky peed his pants immediately. Just as he noticed that Lucy had ran away, he could feel the hot urine flowing into his shoes. Both Mary and the alien continued to stare at him, until the boy sprinted away and was out of sight.

"You better run!" Mary proclaimed, before hugging the alien. The alien felt even colder than it did earlier. Mary realized she should start a fire as soon as she could, before the ominous dark clouds rolled in.

Chapter Fifteen

Still rattled by her confrontation with Susan Webb, Margaret decided to head into town to grocery shop. Although she didn't have much money, buying things always calmed her nerves. No, shopping for groceries wasn't glamourous, but she was looking forward to buying food for dinner without anyone telling her what to get, or complaining that she spent too much or bought the wrong kind of beer.

Margaret took a grocery cart out of its metal stall. Its handle was hot to the touch from sitting in the sun all morning. It was raining ever so slightly, but each raindrop evaporated instantly on the hot asphalt. Margaret waved her hands over the cart for a moment in attempt to cool it down, before lifting George into the buggy bench.

The cart's wheels squeaked and wobbled as she pushed the cart across the parking lot. *Of course, I had to grab the one with the bad wheel.* Margaret knew she could have turned around and gotten a shopping cart without a broken wheel, but her enthusiasm was already waning and she was growing increasingly eager to get this shopping trip over and done with.

Margaret felt judged as soon as she walked through the grocery store's doors. It was if she had a sixth sense. Douglas used to tell her that it was all in her head and that "People are too worried about themselves to judge you," but deep-down Margaret knew that the majority of the townspeople in Falkland did not like her. She could feel it deep in her gut.

Margaret picked up a box of cereal from the shelf, before noticing the price. "That much for cereal? It's just wheat!"

"Can I have some, mama?" George asked.

Maybe she was questioning her harsh parenting methods because of her earlier run in with Susan, or maybe she was just tired of turning everything into a fight, but Margaret shrugged and passed the box of cereal to George. He smiled happily, as he excitedly opened the Cheerios like they were a birthday present. Margaret began to feel oddly emotional. *It is too early for menopause, right?*

Margaret turned to the other woman that she was sharing the grocery store aisle with and smirked. *See, I'm a decent mother.*

A few aisles, and a much fuller cart later, Margaret and George found themselves at the butcher section of the store. It was staffed by a grizzled old butcher who could have passed for an obese version of Friedrich, and his strapping young apprentice who was clearly new to the world of animal slaughter. The cooler was full of all sorts of cuts of meat. Beef tenderloin, rump roast, lamb shanks... She stared for a moment, unsure of what to buy for dinner. She debated asking the handsome young man for a suggestion.

Margaret was so used to cooking Friedrich's tough and often pellet riddled game, that she genuinely wasn't sure which cuts of meat were good anymore. Although she supposed that anything that the butcher sold was going to be better than what she had cooked in quite some time.

"Meat looks so gross," George piped up.

"It's not gross. You're made of meat too, you know," Margaret snapped.

She immediately regretted saying that, and not just because she hated the sounds George made when he cried. Even she knew that comparing a toddler to the meat at the butcher was probably inappropriate. After all, some of the meat on display was especially grotesque; Margaret always wondered who would willingly eat pigs' feet, outside of wartime?

The tall, dark, and handsome butcher's apprentice left his cutting board and walked into the freezer. Margaret began to feel indignant. *He must have seen me upset my son. He knows that I am a terrible mother! Maybe he hates my clothes?* Margaret never considered that he didn't even notice her, and simply went to the freezer because he needed to. *I'm so sick of pretty people judging me,* Margaret agonized internally, falling into her usual thought process.

Never one to pass up the opportunity to talk up a lone lady, Friedrich's fatter doppelganger walked up to the counter. "What can I get you, ma'am?" The butcher asked.

Still incensed by her perceived slight, Margaret decided to make a point. She leaned as close to the counter as she could get without smudging the glass and looked at the old butcher flirtatiously. "Randolph, is it?" Margaret cooed, while reading his name tag.

"That it is."

"I'm trying to think of dinner plans for me and my son, but I'm plain bamboozled! What is your favourite cut of meat?"

A few fake laughs and several free steaks later, Margaret rolled her shopping cart up to the cashier. She placed each item on the counter, including George's partially eaten box of Cheerios, while making severe eye contact with the teenaged employee. This box of cereal was opened already. I'd like a discount."

The cashier looked at Margaret with disappointment, before removing the cereal from the total bill. Margaret was a notorious hassle to serve, and the cashier didn't want any problems. Knowing which customers were trouble was a benefit, or downside, to living in a small town. It depended which side of the cash register you were on.

Chapter Sixteen

Monday, June 23rd

Howling winds and rain had battered the forest Saturday night and all through Sunday. The tarp that Mary had strung up above her makeshift bed stayed surprisingly still, thanks to Mary's excellent knot making skills. However, it kept filling with water. Sensing that the unwell alien needed sleep more than she did, Mary kept an eye on the tarp throughout the night, standing up occasionally to dump out the growing pool that was hanging over their heads.

While things had since settled down, the storm had kept Mary awake for most of the last two nights. She was exhausted. The darkness of the forest wasn't helping, either. The forest was blanketed in heavy dark clouds, which kept out most of the sunlight. Mary needed to get to school though. She debated waking up the alien to tell it she was going, but figured that it was best to let it sleep. Mary tucked the alien under the blanket and kissed it gently on its forehead.

Once at school, Mary had the sinking realization that she hadn't completed her end of year solar system diorama project.

In fact, with all the hecticness of living in the woods and trying to help the alien she hadn't even started it. She stood alone under a large oak tree in the front of the school for a moment, scrambling to think of a plan.

For the first time in her life, Mary was happy to see Lucy, Don, and Ricky approaching. It was a long shot, Mary thought, but there was no way that she was going to fail her class. Summoning all the courage that she could, Mary took a deep breath, held her head high, and walked towards her bullies with the confidence of a protagonist from one of Andrew Allan's Stage shows on CBC radio. Plus, more dark clouds were rolling in, so if Mary got teary-eyed, she figured that she could pretend it was rain.

Lucy and Ricky shrunk down as soon as they spotted Mary approaching. Don looked at them with confusion. If this was some new game that they thought up to torment Mary, he wasn't understanding it.

"Hey loser," Don called out.

"Shut. Up." Lucy growled.

"What? Why? It's just Mary. Baaa—" Ricky elbowed Don in the ribs, mid sheep impression.

"Hi, Mary," Lucy said as kindly as she could. Ricky tipped his hat, as if Mary was a dignitary.

Even though Lucy's words and Ricky's actions came across as even more sarcastic than usual, Mary appreciated that the bullies were at least trying not to upset her. It wasn't the respect that she would rather receive, but in that moment, she figured it would have to do.

"I need your help with something," Mary spoke cautiously. While her words were soft, she kept her head high.

"Do… do you want my diorama? It's yours if you want it," Lucy bargained.

"Mine too!" Ricky blurted out.

"No, I'm not going to steal your work," Mary said with apprehension.

"Then what do you want?" Lucy replied with a less polite tone. As afraid as she was of the alien, and by extension, Mary, she could only pretend to be nice for so long. Mary needed to hurry up.

"Things have been a little weird lately, as I uh, think you know. Could you put my name on your project and tell Miss Webb that we made it together?" Mary offered.

"Wait guys, I didn't think that these were group projects?" Don asked, causing Ricky to elbow him once more.

"Whatever you want, Mary. I'll tell teach that we worked on it together, but that you did most of the work," Lucy submitted.

"Thank you, Lucy. That is very nice of you."

Ricky passed Mary a pencil, which she used to etch her name alongside Lucy's on the bottom of a paper mâché sun. Don remained confused by the entire ordeal. Mary left the bullies, content, and walked into school. As soon as she made it through the front door of the schoolhouse, the ominous black clouds opened up and it began to pour.

Mary walked into Ms. Webb's classroom and took a seat. The class was full of various space-themed decorations and dioramas, including a large banner that read "Congratulations on a year well done!" which was stretched across the chalk board. Head still held high, Mary stared out of the window, concerned about the second wave of storm clouds that were coming in.

As soon as school wrapped for the year, report cards were handed out, and everyone said their goodbyes for the season, Mary sprinted out of the school and back to camp. She wished that she could have spent more time talking with Ms. Webb, but she couldn't squash a sinking feeling that was building in her stomach.

Back at camp, the alien was awake, but it had not moved from where it had slept. Mary approached it with apprehension. "I'm sorry I had to leave you. Did you get enough sleep?"

The alien looked at Mary, wearily.

"Well... I have some good news. I got my final marks from class?" Mary cleared her throat and put on an authoritative voice. "B plus! While not the same caliber of her usual projects, Mary gets bonus marks for going out of her way to help a struggling peer. Mary was a joy to teach, and I can't wait to see how she does next fall in fourth grade!" Mary giggled, and looked to the alien for approval.

The alien looked at her, sadly, and closed its eyes.

"You don't look well."

The alien groaned.

"No, you're still pretty. I mean that you look ill."

Mary examined the alien's bandages. The sites of the alien's injuries were inflamed. Mary had tried to keep the wounds as clean as she could, but only had iodine for disinfectant.

"Let's stay at my house tonight. It's getting late, so mom should be asleep by the time we get there. We'll sneak in."

And so, Mary wrapped her arm around the alien's bony torso, and propped its body up against hers. This was going to be a long walk.

Chapter Seventeen

After several exhausting hours, Mary and the alien eventually reached the Schmidt house. The journey between the forest and the house never usually took that long, but the previous day's storm had flooded patches of the farmer's field, making it nearly impossible for Mary to spot the gopher holes. Some puddles were deceptively deep because of this, and even worse, were tripping hazards. As Mary had to support the alien during the entire walk, she had to be extremely careful not to trip or to lead through any of the dangerous puddles. The alien's health was deteriorating fast; tripping and falling in the wet soggy field would have been a death sentence.

Inside the house, Margaret and her date, the old butcher Randolph, were lying in bed. Randolph's snoring made it impossible for Margaret to get much shut eye. She watched him with disgust as his fat chest, covered only by a ratty stained undershirt, went up and down with each breath. His snoring was something awful, like if someone had put mud in a blender. Maybe gravel. Margaret continued to stare at Randolph for some time before eventually realizing that sleep would not be in the cards for her this night.

Mary stood outside of her bedroom window. She was happy that her eyes had adjusted to the dark so quickly, because it was pitch black outside. At least it wasn't stormy at the moment. She paused though, stumped about how she was going to open this window without the help of her little brother. She knew that George would help if she woke him up, but really felt that it was best to leave him out of this. Suddenly, Mary had an idea.

"I'll be right back," Mary assured the alien, who was resting against the house's rough stucco exterior.

Mary quickly ran to the other side of the house and retrieved a large piece of firewood. The slivers jabbed her fingers and prickled her inner arms as she carried it. She placed it underneath of the bedroom window. It was still going to be a struggle to climb through the window, but at least now she could reach it.

"This is going to be tricky. We need to be quiet..." Mary whispered while putting her hands under the alien's feet. It didn't have toes, which Mary found interesting, as if the alien was wearing transparent shoes.

"On the count of two... One... Two!"

Mary lifted the alien through the bedroom window the best she could. She heard a thud as it landed, which wasn't reassuring, but was relieved when the alien stood up and looked back down at her. She climbed back up on the piece of wood and tried to pull herself into the house. Unfortunately, Mary's arms were strained from half-carrying the alien across of the farmer's field. And she sure as heck wasn't going to ask her declining one-handed friend to lift her up.

"Hang on, I'll be right there!" Mary half-hollered.

She wanted to be as quiet as she could, but her trepidation about bringing the alien into her mother's home was beginning to betray her air of confidence.

Mary ran around to the front of the house as quickly as she could. She nervously placed her hand on the latch of the screen door. She took a deep breath and tried to steady herself, but the combination of stress and exhaustion was making her hands shake. As slowly as she could, Mary pushed the door open.

Creeeeeeeeeeeeeeek.

Oh no. Just then the lights turned on, revealing the frightening figure of Margaret holding a baseball bat. Mary was surprised she still had that. She hadn't seen that thing since her mom pulled her out of little league last summer.

"Mary Louis! Where in Sam Hell—" Margaret screamed. "Mom! I can explain—"

"Shush your mouth. I know what you're doing here." "I just—" Mary stammered.

"You got cold and chickened out of camping," Margaret said, shaking her head. "I knew you didn't have it in you."

"I'm, uh, sorry."

"Just take off your dirty shoes and get to bed. We'll talk about your punishment for waking me up in the morning."

Mary slowly took off her soggy shoes. Her toes were so waterlogged that she wasn't sure they would ever dry out. Margaret winced when she saw her daughter's feet.

"Walk softly. Randolph is trying to sleep," Margaret called out once Mary was halfway down the hall.

"Who is Randolph?" Mary whispered.

"Your mom's new friend. Now hush up and get to bed."

Mary could hear whispers from outside of her bedroom door. She opened it apprehensively to find George sitting in on the floor with the alien.

"Are you real?" George asked while looking at the alien curiously.

The alien blinked slowly and deliberately, as if to assure George yes, it was real, and that this was not a dream.

"Can I touch you?"

The alien reached towards George and gently placed its non-injured hand in his. "Wow," George responded, awe-struck.

"Hey George," Mary said with a hushed voice as she crouched down next to her brother.

"Mary! You're home!" George exclaimed while giving her a huge enthusiastic hug. "I want you to meet my new friend," he naively offered while gesturing to the alien.

"Yes, we've met. George, this is the friend that I was camping with. They're not doing well though, and I don't know what to do to help."

"Maybe they just need a good night's sleep? Naps make me feel better when I am sad."

"That's a good idea, Georgie."

With the help of her brother, Mary managed to lift the alien off the floor and led it towards her bed. The alien plopped down on to the springy mattress, which elicited a yell and a knock through their mother's bedroom wall. "Keep it down in there!" Margaret shouted, causing Randolph to groan and rollover in his sleep.

Mary placed her pillow underneath the alien's large head. She pulled up the knit blankets and tucked them in the best that she could. She placed another blanket over the alien's feet, which stuck out comically over the edge of the too small bed. George looked to Mary intently and asked, "Do you have Mr. Purdy with you?"

As luck would have it, Mary had packed up Mr. Purdy as well as a few of the other essential things from the camp before she left. She picked the damp teddy bear up out of her bag and passed it to George. George, in turn, gave the bear to the alien. "This will help you sleep," George spoke solemnly.

"You should go back to sleep too, Georgie. It's way past your bedtime."

"But I want to stay awake with you!"

"I know, but we've got to be careful not to wake up Mom and her new friend."

George reluctantly crawled into his bed. "I don't like Mom's new friend," George confessed as Mary tucked him in. "Why is Mama always friends with cruel people?"

"I wish I knew. Maybe we'll understand when we are adults."

Mary returned to the alien's side and watched it with concern. She placed the back of her hand on its head but was unable to tell if the alien had gotten any colder or not. She didn't know if aliens got fevers in the first place! This was all so frustrating. The already exhausted Mary started to feel those hot tears building up behind her eyes again.

"You're cold. But I don't know if this is normal. How do you feel?"

The alien made a few weak clicking noises.

Click... click....

Chapter Eighteen

Struggling to fall back to sleep after her run in with Mary, Margaret decided to wrap around Randolph, who was sleeping soundly – albeit, quite noisily – in her bed. His pockmarked nose released a snore as loud as a jet engine every time his fat chest inhaled and exhaled. No, he wasn't Margaret's type physically, or even personality-wise. But Randolph was no worse than Friedrich. At least, not that Margaret knew. And besides, he had a paying job. Margaret placed her thin but muscular arm over Randolph's chest, and placed her feet against his legs.

"Jesus, woman! What's wrong with you?! Your feet are freezing!" Randolph blurted out.

"I'm sorry—" Margaret apologized.

She honestly hadn't meant to wake him.

"Enough! Your sorries won't put me back to sleep!"

"Just close your eyes and I'm sure you'll be back to sleep in no time," Margaret offered, as sing-songy as she could.

Suddenly, Margaret and Randolph could hear crying coming from the kids' bedroom.

"What is that sound?"

"Oh, Mary came home a bit ago."

"Who's Mary?" Randolph asked, puzzled.

"My kid."

"I thought its name was Greg?"

"George is my son, the one you met. I've got a daughter, too." Margaret began to wish that she had conversed more with Randolph before inviting him over.

"You've got two kids?! When were you gonna tell me?!" Randolph said accusingly while springing out of bed. He stood over Margaret in only his stained formerly white under- shirt and briefs.

"I guess I just forgot—"

"You were trying to trick me!" Randolph shouted, while wagging his finger in Margaret's face. Maybe he was just as bad as Friedrich after all.

"I truly wasn't..." Margaret offered.

Even though he was clearly repulsive – Margaret wasn't blind – she really hoped that Randolph wouldn't leave. It was difficult enough to get her second husband to marry her.

"Well if I'm going to be with a woman with two kids, they better at least learn to be quiet and to respect that the man of the house needs his sleep!" Randolph grabbed his pair of trousers from the floor, but rather than putting them on, proceeded to pull the belt out of the loops.

"It's fine. Just lay back down and go back to sleep."

Randolph ignored Margaret, and stormed towards Mary and George's bedroom with his belt in hand. Margaret let out a tired sigh and followed him.

No longer crying, Mary was now sitting on the side of her bed. She was gently holding her portable radio next to the alien's head and was playing *Twinkle Twinkle Little Star* as quietly as the radio would allow. Just as the song reached its final verse, and the alien began to fall asleep, Randolph burst through the bedroom door, in all his half-dressed rage.

"Now listen here, missy—"

"I can explain!" Mary blurted out instinctively, before fully realizing that this man was a stranger, and clearly unhinged.

And with that, the alien sat-up and let out a terrifying scream. Despite the alien's failing health, it managed to shriek even louder than it had earlier.

"Sweet baby Jesus," Randolph murmured, while peeing in his already disgusting tighty-whities. From the other side of the bedroom, George tried as hard as he could to stay quiet and not giggle.

"What is going on?" Margaret asked in her usual inflammatory tone, while stepping in front of Randolph. As she took in the sight of the injured alien in her daughter's bed, she let out the loudest, most blood-curdling scream that Mary had ever heard. "OH MY GOD! MARY! WHAT IS THAT?!" Margaret wailed as she stared directly into the alien's eyes.

Sensing the obvious hostility, the alien dragged itself out of bed, and began to carry its weak frame towards the window. Even hunched over, its stature dwarfed everyone in the room. Margaret and Randolph backed up and were cowering in the doorway.

"Mary, George… Get over here," Margaret whispered.

"Mom, it's fine."

"Now is not the time to argue, Mary!"

The alien feebly tried to open the bedroom window. Despite its height, there was such a fragility to its movements. The alien's struggle to open the window reminded Mary of a crane fly stuck on the wrong side of the screen door. "I'm not leaving it! We're friends!"

Attempting to retake control of the situation, while still in his soiled undergarments, Randolph stepped towards Mary with his belt in hand. "Don't you dare talk back to your mother like that."

The alien abandoned its attempt to open the window, and stepped in front of Mary protectively. It let out a low grumble that Mary hadn't heard before.

"I'm calling the police!" Margaret yelled before running away, with Randolph right behind her.

Mary turned to the alien and looked into its large brown eyes. In that moment she was so deeply afraid. She had only brought the alien home to heal, and now she had made everything worse.

"We need to get you out of here!" Mary said, while pulling the alien back towards the window.

"Should I come too?" George asked.

"Stay here, and hide under the covers," Mary pleaded. She wasn't entirely sure why she thought her brother should hide, but that sinking feeling she started having yesterday hadn't gone away.

Fortunately, it was easier to use the window as an escape than as an entrance. Both Mary and the alien landed on the ground, making two separate thuds. The soggy grass acted as a cushion. Mary wrapped her arm around the alien and propped it up once again. "Come on, let's go..." Mary said as encouragingly as she could to the alien.

The two of them moved inches at a time, slowly sinking into the muddy backyard. To make matters worse, it was starting to rain again.

"Get back here Mary! Leave that thing alone!" Margaret screamed from the doorstep of the house.

Mary looked over her shoulder and back at her mother. After several minutes, Mary and the alien had barely been able to reach the field.

"We've got to keep going. Please, just a bit further. I believe in you—" Mary pleaded with the failing alien.

As the alien collapsed onto the soggy earth, Randolph sprinted out of the house, now wrapped up in one of Margaret's floral housecoats and carrying on of Friedrich's hunting rifles, making much better time than his frame would suggest. "Out of the way, girly," Randolph ordered, pushing Mary out of the way with the barrel of the gun.

"No! Don't hurt it! We're friends!" Mary prayed, stepping between the shotgun and the alien.

"No one is friends with a monster," Randolph said, not understanding the irony of his words. "Now move!"

"No!" Mary roared.

In that moment, half of a second slowed down to what felt like an eternity. Using its good arm, the alien pulled Mary to its side, and out of the way of the shotgun blast. The alien collapsed, gasping. Randolph had not picked up the pellet gun by mistake, as Mary was hoping he had. Having been hit just under its neck, the alien's chest was torn open from the close range force of the blast.

"No, no, no! Please don't die," Mary pleaded while trying to stop the bleeding. Her hands looked especially small in the moment, as she tried to plug the wound in the alien's chest. "I can't lose you. You're my only friend. Please, please don't leave me here."

The alien took Mary's hands off of its chest and held them tightly in its singular fist. It let out a few soft clicks, while gesturing to a spot in the northern corner of the sky with its other arm. It looked Mary intensely in the eyes and communicated something that only she was to know, before the light faded from its large eyes.

By now, the rain had turned into a torrential downpour. Mary leaned over the alien and gave it one final hug. Covered in an awful mixture of mud and blood, Mary lunged at Randolph with all the force that her nine-year-old body could muster.

"How could you do that? I hate you! I hate you so much! I wish you were dead!" Mary screamed and wailed while kicking and punching Randolph.

Unsure of how to respond, Randolph pushed Mary off of him and tried his best to keep her at arm's length.

Finally leaving the safety of the doorstep, Margaret ran over and grabbed Mary, trying her best to keep her away from Randolph.

"Let me go! You're as bad as he is!" Mary continued to yell while trying to escape her mother's grasp.

Chapter Nineteen

Thursday, July 3ʳᵈ

Once again, Mary was sitting at her bedroom window. Her head in her hands, with her elbows propped up on the ledge of the windowsill. The inner parts of her arms were pink with sunburn as she hardly moved from this spot. George had begun to tease Mary that she was turning into a houseplant. Today was the third of July. Nearly two weeks had passed since the alien was shot in front of Mary. Nearly two weeks had passed since she placed her hands on its chest to stop the bleeding. Nearly two weeks had passed since Mary last looked her mother in the eyes…

While Mary admittedly didn't understand the complicated world of adult relationships, she found it disturbing that her mother was still seeing the man that had murdered Mary's best friend. At least Mary assumed that her mother was, anyway. Mary hadn't left her bedroom, except to use the washroom.

"I brought you a snack," George whispered, while sliding Mary a plate with a piece of cake.

"Thank you," Mary muttered, without shifting her gaze.

George watched his sister for a moment, before leaving.

Mary looked down at the piece of vanilla sheet cake. It was primarily white, with little bits of red and blue icing. When intact, the cake had read "Happy Dominion Day!" Mary's current piece just had "ay!" on it, which felt much more celebratory than she was currently comfortable with. While Mary hadn't attended the party, she had watched her family attend the neighbourhood's Dominion Day celebrations from afar. She poked at the cake with disinterest, before picking up the fork and taking a bite. The cake wasn't terrible, but it was starting to dry out, as it had most likely been left on the counter since the party happened two days ago.

Mary swallowed the cake. It was dry and stuck as it went down her throat. She momentarily debated leaving her room to get a glass of milk but didn't feel up to that yet. She pushed the plate of cake away and continued to stare outdoors. If Mary closed her eyes, she could imagine that the clicks of the grasshoppers were coming from the alien.

Later, as dusk was approaching, George came back into the bedroom. "Mom is mad you missed dinner." Understanding his sister's silence, George sat next to Mary and placed his head on her shoulder. Mary looked over at her little brother and placed his hand in hers.

Mary awoke in the middle of the night to find that she had fallen asleep looking out the window. She looked over at George, who was fast asleep in his bed. It made her slightly sad that he no longer needed her to tuck him in at night. She stood up and placed her bare feet on the coarsely carpeted floor, which felt like standing on a bed of nails. Apparently sitting in one spot for that long could make someone quite sore. After eventually shaking the pins and needles feeling out of her feet, Mary finally decided to leave her bedroom.

No longer caring if she woke anyone up, Mary walked down the hall. The faded pink walls of the hallway were strewn with framed old photos from happier times. Photos of a smiling Margaret holding George and Mary as babies. A drawing that Mary made when she was in kindergarten. An old family photo with Mary's late father, Douglas, holding George as a baby in the hospital. Mary wasn't sure if this picture was from when George was a newborn, or if it was from when their dad was in the hospital at the beginning of his cancer treatment. Sometimes Mary would stop and stare at these old photos. Stopping to trace the old images with her finger, as if she could still reach out and touch her father. As if the picture was a portal into happier times. Tonight though, Mary did not feel like looking at the photos.

Out of habit, Mary still caught herself dodging the squeaky spots on the floor. It wasn't because she was worried about her mother's wrath, though. at this point Mary didn't care about anything. No one could do or say anything to her that would make her feel any worse. What was her mother going to do? Yell at her for waking up Randolph again? Nothing mattered anymore.

The closer that Mary got to the kitchen, the more that she could feel the vibration of the refrigerator on her feet. While the humming of the refrigerator was usually overpowered by daytime atmospheric sounds, conversations or more often than not someone yelling, at night the mechanical rumblings of the fridge were quite noticeable.

With only the moon lighting her path, Mary found her way into the kitchen. She opened the cupboard that was next to the fridge, grabbed a glass, and poured herself some milk. The stale cake that she had eaten earlier was most certainly digested by now, but the milk was still refreshing. As Mary finished drinking the glass of milk, she spotted the faint glow of a lit cigarette from someone sitting at the kitchen table.

"Everyone thinks that this family is a freak show," Margaret muttered.

Mary stood in place, frozen.

"While you were out having your little adventure, I was trying to keep a roof over your little brother's head. Not that you care though, you unappreciative brat." Margaret took a deep pull on the cigarette and let out a phlegmy cough. Mary remained still, hoping that if she went long enough without speaking that her Mother would get bored and leave her alone. "Do you think things have been easy for me since your father left?"

"He didn't leave, he died," Mary attested.

"Same thing."

"Dad didn't want to leave us. He was sick. I remember."

"Can't you ever just nod and smile and agree with what I am saying? Why'd you always have to be so combative?" Margaret ashed her cigarette in a coffee cup and stood up. She teetered ever so slightly as she looked down at Mary. Mary wasn't certain, but it looked like her mother had been drinking. This was especially jarring to Mary, since she knew how much her mother typically hated liquor.

"Apologize to me," Margaret slurred.

Mary continued to stare back at her mother. She knew whatever she said to her was going to be misinterpreted, so she figured that it was best to remain silent. Margaret took another deep drag from the cigarette.

"I didn't want Randolph to kill your friend, you know." Margaret picked up the coffee cup off the table and mashed her cigarette into it. "We all make mistakes," Margaret muttered, as she turned and walked warily down the hallway, leaving Mary alone in the dark kitchen.

Chapter Twenty

Tuesday, July 8ᵗʰ

Just as she had spent every day that week, Mary was once again sitting by her bedroom window. Sometimes her gaze would wander, and she would catch herself watching other kids playing on the street. Mary wasn't watching them with any sort of jealousy or envy though; she didn't feel that she was missing out on anything by not being their friend. She mostly watched them with curiosity. Ever since Mary befriended the alien, regular life felt surreally mundane. *How can everyone act like everything is normal when there are aliens out there?* Mary would wonder. Sometimes that curiosity would shift to anger though, as she also couldn't understand how life seemed to continue as normal even though someone so important to her just died. Mary felt as if her emotions were on a pendulum.

While Mary sat quietly by the window, Margaret and Randolph would occasionally place their head against her bedroom door to listen it. They wanted to know why exactly she spent all day, every day, looking out of that damn window.

The only option they didn't consider was to ask Mary how she was feeling.

"Your girl isn't right," Randolph mumbled to Margaret, with a hint of disgust in his voice.

"She's in mourning," Margaret empathized.

"Over that freak? I did her a favour."

"She's my daughter, not yours. Let me worry about this." Margaret rebutted.

"Whatever, woman." Randolph left his spot outside of Mary's room, and stomped down the hall like an oversized and unwashed petulant child.

That was it. Margaret was sick of this behaviour. She was tired of people disrespecting her. She couldn't even get her own daughter to speak to her anymore, and now this low-life that only made her relationships with her children worse was talking down to her? True, he had a good paying job, and Margaret had no idea how she would support her family without a man, but she had finally reached her breaking point.

"Don't talk to me like that," Margaret spoke with an authoritative tone that she wasn't sure if she had ever directed at a man before.

Randolph froze in his tracks. "You're certainly uppity. Where's this coming from?"

"I think you should leave."

"Make me," Randolph replied with a disgusting grin.

Margaret eyed the baseball bat that she kept sitting by the front door of the house but decided to solve things with words this time. Margaret was amazed at just how much power the words "I am going to report you for slaughtering illegally hunted animals" had over the old butcher. The contact information that the Conservation Officers gave her a few weeks earlier turned out to be surprisingly useful.

While George was mostly focused on colouring at the time and wasn't quite sure why Randolph left the house so quickly, he knew that this was good news, and had to share it with his sister. He ran down the hallway as quickly as his little legs would take him and hopped up next to Mary who was still seated at the bedroom window. George breathed deeply, to catch his breath after running there so quickly.

"Good news! Mom made her friend leave. I didn't like him," George said with a gasp. "Mary?" George lightly tapped on Mary's shoulder. She had fallen asleep. He walked over to her bed and grabbed the comforter off it. He dragged the large blanket across the room and draped it over his sister's shoulders.

Having once again missed dinner, Mary woke up from her windowsill nap long past nightfall. She breathed deeply and filled her lungs with the gentle summer night air. The sky was pitch black and strewn with stars. She noticed the blanket wrapped around her, and her little brother sleeping soundly in his own bed. In that moment, everything was quiet. Even the crickets were asleep.

Mary walked over to George's bed, and gave him a kiss on the forehead. Even though he was so young, she was grateful that George was always there for her. And then, for the first time since she lost her friend, Mary smiled.

Suddenly, Mary spotted something out of the corner of her eye. *What was that?* Mary jumped up and ran back towards the window. The remnants of a bright blue streak floated in the atmosphere for a few seconds, before fading completely. Even though she hadn't seen the ship clearly, Mary knew deep down in her gut what had happened. She ran back to George, and gently shook him awake.

"George! Psst! Georgie! Wake up!"

"What is it, Mary?" George said groggily, while rubbing his eyes.

"They're here!"

"Who's here?"

"The alien's friends! I think they've come back to look for it," Mary exclaimed before running to the window. "I need to go and tell them what happened!"

"Can I come?" George asked innocently, even though he knew what his sister would say.

"George…"

"I understand. Please come home after," George bargained. "I will."

"Promise?"

George held up his tiny pinky finger. The two of them pinky swore, earnestly.

"I love you so much George. I've got to hurry though!"

Without hesitation, Mary grabbed her bag and hopped back out of the bedroom window.

Chapter Twenty-One

Mary landed on the ground with a thud, and as soon as her feet hit the ground, she burst into a full speed sprint across the backyard and towards the forest. While she didn't see where the flying saucer had landed, she had a hunch that the aliens would be going to the quarry to look for their fallen compatriot. Falkland was a tiny town, where else would they have wanted to go? Mary wanted to be the first to reach the spaceship; she didn't trust any adults to handle the situation as well as she could.

Sensing that something was amiss, Margaret went into Mary and George's bedroom to check on her children. Noticing that Mary's bed was empty, Margaret went up to George, who was staring out the window, entranced.

"Where the hell is your sister?" Margaret demanded, with her hands on her hips.

"She went to tell them what happened to her friend," George explained, while pointing forebodingly into the distance.

"Wait. Tell who what?"

"The spacemen, Mom!" George exclaimed, exasperatedly.

Margaret bolted out of the bedroom, leaving her young son once again abandoned by the window.

Mary ran through the forest at full speed. By now she had memorized many of the hazards along the way. She knew where certain hills started, and which rocks were loose and not reliable to climb on. While her focus was on getting the quarry as quickly as she could, Mary couldn't help but have fun running through the deep dark forest now that she was no longer afraid.

At last, Mary reached the side of the quarry. Just as she had imagined, the flying saucer had landed square in the middle of the pit. Mary watched closely, as the ship's door slowly opened. Noticing lights from police cars approaching, Mary threw caution to the wind, slid down the quarry embankment, and ran towards the ship as quickly as she could. By the time Mary got to the bottom of the slope, she spotted two aliens, nearly identical to her friend, exiting the ship.

Mary waved frantically at the aliens. They looked at one another, then to Mary, and then back to one another. *What is this weird small animal trying to signal?* With the police cars now parked along the side of the quarry, Mary knew that she had to act quickly. She kept her arms in the air, trying her best to signal that she was not a threat to the aliens.

"I knew your friend! I tried to help!"

Sensing that running towards the aliens might be seen as a threat, she tried her best to slow down and walk more benevolently. Mary moved closer and closer before, without warning, she felt a slight jolt go throughout her body. It wasn't painful, just an odd feeling. It was as if she stepped through some sort of force field and was now on the other side of it. Mary now stood almost face to face with the two aliens. Or face to waist more accurately. If Mary had to guess she would have said that they were seven to eight feet tall; just slightly taller than the alien that she had befriended. Only just over four feet tall, Mary was especially tiny next to these beings.

Understanding that this child was no danger to them, the taller of the two aliens let out a series of rapid clicks while the second placed its hand on Mary's forehead. Mary closed her eyes, and in that moment understood everything the aliens wanted her to know. There was a brief yet beautiful moment of serenity, before six uniformed members of the British Columbia Provincial Police surrounded Mary and the aliens.

"Little girl, step away from the, um, not so little green men," The lead officer called out.

"Of all the things you thought you'd say today huh, Bill?" The officer nearest to him joked under his breath.

Mary turned away from the aliens and towards the police officers, and noticed her mother standing next to the officer she assumed was in charge. "They're not here to hurt anybody. They just came to rescue their friends, who crashed here earlier," Mary called out as she watched as the crowd of officers slowly got closer and closer. "I had to tell them that one of their friends died in the crash, and that the other died because... Because of adults like you." Mary looked at her mom, who was now whispering something to the lead officer.

"Listen here, missy. This is official government business.

Go back to your mother!" The lead officer commanded. "Mary! I just want you to come home so I can bake you

some cookies and give you a hug…" Margaret trailed off, realizing that Mary could clearly tell she was lying.

"Ah, who am I kidding. GET YOUR BUTT BACK OVER HERE NOW, OR YOU ARE GROUNDED ALL SUMMER!" Margaret belted.

"Jeez…" Several of the officers muttered to themselves. Mary turned back towards the aliens.

"Please take me with you. I am useful. I can cook, I can clean…" Mary pleaded.

The aliens looked to one another, uneasily. The pupils in their large eyes fluctuated in size.

"You have until the count of three to step away from the ship! You don't know what these creatures are capable of. They could be dangerous!" The lead officer said, while gesturing to his team to ready their weapons.

Mary grabbed on to one of the alien's hands and looked into its understanding eyes.

"Don't leave me here."

"ONE!"

"Take me with you."

"TWO!"

"Please."

"I'm so serious, lassie," The officer called out, without a tinge of hesitation.

Just as Mary turned around and looked back at the officers, the commanding officer twisted his finger in the air, signalling his men to fire.

"THREE!"

Exactly as promised, all six officers opened fire on the aliens. Mary winced, expecting the worse to happen. She kept her eyes closed and braced herself. It was only when she couldn't hear any bullets ricocheting off the ship, that Mary opened her eyes. The force field that Mary had walked through was somehow absorbing the bullets! The aliens put their arms around Mary protectively as the three of them watched the bullets that were being fired at them seemingly disappear into thin air.

As the aliens turned to lead Mary up the ramp into their ship, the officers stopped firing. Mary wasn't sure if they were stunned by everything that they had witnessed, or if it was simply because they had run out of ammunition.

"Mary, get back here! You can't go with them!" Margaret called out as she began to run towards the ship. "I know I'm lousy sometimes, but I need you at home," Margaret confessed as she walked through the force field.

Mary wondered if her mom was going to try to board the ship. As Margaret got closer though, her mood shifted once again, offended that Mary didn't immediately turn and run into her arms. "You know what? Leave! I don't care!" Margaret screamed, while taking off her shoes.

Margaret hurled the first shoe at the side of the spaceship, the second one hit the larger of the two aliens in the back of the head. Both aliens froze in place. The alien that was hit by the shoe clapped its gangly hands together, and using some unseen force, flung both shoes back out into the crowd. Margaret seethed as the judgemental aliens continued onto the ship, ignoring her.

Once Mary and the aliens were on board, the loading ramp slowly folded back into the ship, while the door began to close. As the door closed, the officers once again opened fired on the ship, this time hitting it. The bullets bounced off the ship like hail. Mary turned and looked back at her mother through the diminishing opening in the door. The flying saucer began to glow bright blue, before jetting off into space at hyper speed.

George continued sitting at his bedroom window, staring off into the distance with his cardboard telescope. When he spotted the magnificent blue light stream across of the sky, he realized that his sister had left him behind. He knew that Mary would return one day though; she had pinky sworn.

PART TWO

"The beauty of the universe lies in its infinite possibilities and undiscovered truths."

- Art Bell

Chapter One

Tuesday, July 8th (1947)

The sounds of gunfire echoed in Mary's head as the door of the flying saucer closed behind her. *That was close,* she thought to herself as she caught her breath. She imagined the officers on the other side of the door, confused that their bullets were bouncing off the sides of the alien spacecraft. Someone with a weaker constitution might need a moment to accept that they had gone from running across a farmer's field, to the middle of a police shootout, to the inside of a flying saucer all within the span of about thirty minutes. But not Mary! Although she was only nine years old, she had nerves of steel, or at the very least, aluminum.

The saucer's loading ramp folded into the floor, similar to the way an escalator's stairs seemingly disappear. There was no tractor beam involved in Mary's journey into the saucer, no beam at all actually. The spaceship appeared surprisingly simple in its construction. As the concerningly thin metal-like door sealed up behind Mary and her rescuers, she could still hear the ricochet of the British Columbia Provincial Police officer's revolver bullets ping off of the side of the ship, as well as the thud from her mother's second shoe being tossed. Mary looked down at her own dirty shoes and tattered dress and wondered if she was going to be given a spacesuit, but now didn't feel like the appropriate time to ask.

"Are we going to be okay?" Mary questioned as she looked at her two saviours from the sky for comfort. The two aliens peered down at Mary; their lanky bodies shone iridescently as the ship's interior lights reflected off of their blue scaly skin.

You don't need to worry, the first alien seemed to say as it placed its hand on Mary's shoulder, its large doe-like brown eyes locked with hers.

The ship began to hum as it powered up. From the inside, it felt as if the ship was vibrating ever so slightly, almost like the entire ship was alive. Seeing the two aliens remain still during this process kept Mary calm as well. *It is their ship after all, they know what they're doing. If they aren't scared, then I shouldn't be either.* Mary couldn't see the magnificent blue glow that was emitting from the bottom of the ship as it prepared to launch.

✳✳✳

"Take cover!" the lead BCPP officer called out. Like most people in the town, or rather, like most people in the world, his only knowledge of flying saucers was limited to what they talked about in science fiction radio shows. Needless to say, he was quite frightened. Taking his lead, the five other members of the squad all dove behind whatever was nearest to them in the quarry. Out of that group of people, only Mary's mother, Margaret, continued to stand and watch as the saucer zipped off into outer space. That image would be burned in her mind for the rest of her life.

Back at the Schmidt house, Mary's little brother Georgie was peering out his bedroom window. His small toddler frame was pressed against the wooden sill as his nubby fingers held up a paper tube as a telescope. Mary had promised him that she would come home, but when she still hadn't returned by morning, four-year-old Georgie knew that she had left without him.

Chapter Two

Tuesday, July 2nd (1963)

It was the day after Dominion Day, and *Surfin' USA* was blasting from George Schmidt's truck's speakers with enough strength to make it feel as if a miniature Dennis Wilson was drumming inside of his ear canal. Rubbing his temple with his left hand, George hunched forward and turned the radio off with his right as he continued to steer his 1955 fire engine red Chevy pickup with his knees. He always told himself he'd drive more safely if there was a passenger, but since no one ever wanted to ride with him – perhaps partially for this reason – George saw no reason to care. It was fun to barrel down the empty roads on the way to work; sometimes he'd speed up just so the rattles of his truck hitting potholes would sync up with the songs on the radio. George was resigned to speed in silence this morning though, because of his pounding headache.

Like many other nineteen-year-olds in the city of Penticton, British Columbia, George had stayed up a little too late hanging around a beach bonfire the night before. Although some college students rolled their eyes and considered celebrating Dominion Day to be antiquated, sure enough, they would be partying at the beach or going to a barbecue on the first of July, like everyone else. Being situated between two lakes meant that summer was Penticton's time to shine; teenagers there would celebrate the opening of an envelope if it gave them an excuse to hang out and take in the sunshine.

While he didn't have many friends in the city, as a relatively handsome young man, George found it easy enough to meet new people when he went out. It wasn't a struggle for him to make friends at parties; his struggles came with keeping those friends for more than a few weeks. After the disappearance of his sister Mary sixteen years prior, George found he could only present a certain version of himself to the world. He knew that if he ever told people, "My sister was abducted by aliens," they would think he was crazy. It was just simpler for him to keep everyone at arm's reach while he focused on work.

At last, the increasingly bald tires of George's pickup slowed to a crawl as he approached the parking lot of the Dominion Radio Astrophysical Observatory. Just because George was an immature teenager who drove like an idiot, it didn't mean that he wanted his coworkers to know that he was one. Besides, he would be turning twenty soon and wanted them to take him more seriously.

George looked down at his wristwatch, which he was told used to belong to his father, Douglas. He was told his father received it as a gift when he first became an Engineering Officer with the US Army, which was the extent of what George knew about his dad, and the watch. Its leather strap had begun to soften over time, causing the watch to hang slightly off of George's chubby pale wrist. He didn't own much else of his father's, most of those belongings were lost to time, sold off to cover the bills, or given to his older sister, Mary. The hint of acridity that he felt when he imagined Mary spending time with their father surprised George. He and Mary were close when they were children, thicker than thieves. He had no right to be envious of her for having a few more happy memories of their father than George himself had. While Mary was only nine years old when she went missing, she had been George's brave protector during those drunken nights between their mother and whichever suitor she had at the time. Mary was his confidant. His friend. The reason that George had pursued a career in space exploration in the first place. Realizing that he had become lost in thought, George once again looked at his watch. 7:45AM. Dust still lingered in the air as he hopped out of the truck and made his way into the break room with enough time for a pre-work cup of joe.

***

The hot brown liquid scalded the back of George's throat as he took a long swig from a stained ceramic mug which had the Canadian Coat of Arms printed on the side. The coat of arms was on a few of the dishes in the break room, most likely brought back by one of the researchers after a trip to

Ottawa. George only cared about what was in the cup; after the long weekend he had, he needed all of the caffeine that he could get. However, it would be a stretch to refer to this murky water as coffee, seeing as the flavour resembled water that had been wrung through a dirty sponge more than it did actual java. As long as he drank it quickly, and with several sugar cubes, it would at least numb the pounding in his head. Besides, it was free.

"It hurts me to say this, but sometimes free isn't best. That coffee really is awful," George's bespectacled older colleague, Robert, piped up while placing his heavy steel Thermos on the scuffed-up counter. Robert massaged his bony old wrist, which was clearly strained by the weight of the large beverage container, before reaching into the office kitchen cupboard for his own stained ceramic mug to use.

"Get a Thermos – it's the best investment I ever made," Robert spoke whimsically, using his long plaid sleeve to wipe out the bottom of the dusty mug. Robert was cheap, or 'thrifty', as he would say when correcting people. As a young adult on a limited budget, George appreciated that about his coworker.

"Did you have a good long weekend?" George asked, making small talk.

"I did! The kids and I went down to the beach and then we came home and cooked some hot dogs over the fire for lunch," Robert answered. "What about you? Did you go back home to visit your family?"

"Not until next weekend," George replied.

"Ah, that's right. For your late sister's birthday?" Robert added while unscrewing the top of his Thermos. Robert didn't know much about George, but he always tried his best to make him feel accepted.

"Something like that," George answered, attempting to answer as a normal person would, and not as someone who was actually hiding a sixteen-year family secret. Robert was always kind, but it was difficult for George to trust people that he wasn't immediately related to. It was exceedingly hard to make friends while leading such a private life, but he was beginning to grow used to it. George took a sip of his coffee and winced. It really was terrible.

"At the very least, throw some whiskey in next time," Robert said with a friendly wink as he poured a mug of home-brewed coffee, before sealing up the Thermos and leaving the break room.

"Thanks for the advice," George replied sarcastically, knowing Robert was not listening.

After rinsing out his mug and putting it back in its place, George found himself annoyed by Robert's casual whisky comment. He rationalized that his colleague didn't know about his drinking and was only trying to make a friendly joke, but it still got under his skin. Whisky, whisky, whisky… It was all he could think about now. He hated feeling this way.

Although he would never admit to it out loud, George would sometimes catch himself looking to Robert as a father figure. But deep down, his insecurities would never let him pursue a friendship like that. Why would Robert want a son, or even a friend, like him anyway? Unlike Robert, George wasn't a *real* scientist. Or any sort of scientist, actually. He was an administrative assistant. The scientists with proper degrees and experience did all of the research. George merely kept the workstations tidy, printed things, and occasionally brought envelopes containing their findings into town to be shipped to the National Research Council of Canada's head office in Ottawa.

For someone who didn't attend university and who had grown up in a place so small it wasn't officially designated as a town, George was accomplishing more than most thought he was capable of. Heck, his adoptive mother, Susan Webb, was proud of him just for moving out of Falkland, even if it was only to a town two hours away. Some might appreciate the lack of stress that would come with lowered expectations, but it just made George feel weak and small. He wanted people to depend on him – he wanted to be the type of person that his late father would have been proud of!

When he made his annual trip back to Falkland, George smugly enjoyed the shock that once-familiar faces seemed to have when he told them that he was employed by the National Research Council of Canada. At night though, when it was only George and his thoughts, the memories of those shocked faces twisted into faces of pity and mockery. They weren't impressed, they were humouring him. Those faces knew that he was only an assistant, that his career was a farce. And that was when he would turn to a bottle of alcohol.

These days, George lived in Penticton. Located along- side a lake and surrounded by orchards, sometimes it felt like paradise. But George's reason for moving here wasn't for pleasure: his life, and his entire career, had been in hopes of finding out where exactly his sister disappeared to. Penticton was the closest city to the village of Kaleden, which was home to the Dominion Radio Astrophysical Observatory, a research facility that used telescopes to survey the stars and collect solar activity data. He would have lived in Kaleden itself if that was possible, but his budget only allowed for a small apartment in the city. Even though he wasn't actually a scientist and hadn't gone to school to study astrophysics, George had managed to learn quite a bit during the past two years he had spent as an administrative assistant. His hope was that by working closely with the research scientists, he would be the first to know if a UFO was spotted, either by eavesdropping on the scientists or by one of them loudly proclaiming, "We have spotted a UFO!" George imagined that they'd be pretty excited by the discovery.

Over the years George had considered bluntly asking Robert and the other researchers if they knew anything about aliens, but he didn't want them to think that he was nuts. Since no one outside of the family saw what happened to Mary that night – the official story was that she ran away and was probably kidnapped or eaten by wolves – it was difficult to get anyone to listen, let alone believe the story about the UFO. The only person that believed him was his mother, Margaret, but once she was sent away to live in a care home for the mentally invalid, George kept his mouth shut. In the meantime, he would continue to work at the observatory, and secretly print out copies of star charts to use for his own research.

Chapter Three

Tuesday, July 8th (1947) - Stardate 194707.08

While Mary didn't have any past experience with space-ships – although, she supposed, she had as much experience with them than anyone else from Earth – this one felt exceptionally underwhelming. Except for a simple control panel, it didn't appear that the ship contained much else. It was just a plain room with white walls and a few lights. *Rinky dink* was the exact phrase that came to Mary's mind. Although she only ever heard old people use that saying, it was the term that felt the most appropriate. "Where is everything?" Mary asked to neither of the two aliens in particular.

"Where is everything?" the slightly taller of the two repeated, its head cocked questioningly. Mary realized that since the aliens' mouths never seemed to move when they spoke, they must be talking to her psychically, just as the doomed alien she had previously befriended had.

"Yes, where do you sleep? Where do you sit to eat? And..." Mary paused for a moment. "Where is the bathroom?"

Although neither alien's face was capable of showing much expression, they both looked at Mary connoting a sense of bemusement with their faint eyebrow ridges.

"I find it curious that your first question wasn't about who we are, or where we are going," the slightly shorter of the two aliens responded. *"To answer all of your questions, the ship is much larger than what you see here. Come with me and I'll show you everything, including the bathroom."*

Mary nodded and began to follow the alien towards a doorway that seemingly appeared out of nowhere. It wasn't actually that high-tech though; the door was a sliding door that had opened as Mary's back was turned.

"Larry needs to stay here to work his shift in the control centre while I give you the tour," the alien explained as he led Mary to the doorway.

"Larry?" This time Mary was the one who was bemused.

"Technically his name is something that you are unable to comprehend. In our language, it would sound more like a high-pitched shriek to you. So, for the duration of your stay with us, we have chosen to call ourselves by some of your continent's most popular names. You may call me George."

"George is the name of my little brother," Mary noted solemnly. In all of the commotion, she hadn't really considered that she had left him behind.

"What would you prefer to call me?" the alien asked.

"I don't know..." For the first time since boarding the ship, Mary felt anxious. She had never named anyone before. "How about… Geor… gio?" She hoped that it would sound similar enough to his first choice that the alien would not be offended.

"Georgio it is then," Georgio replied.

"I need to know…" Mary trailed off with a sadness in her voice. "What was the name of the alien—" She paused. *Do you call aliens, aliens?* Mary didn't know the proper way to phrase her question, so she blurted it out instead. "What was the name of my friend that died?"

"The young scout that crashed on your planet had chosen the Earth name Ray, in case she needed to introduce herself to anyone," Georgio explained. *"She was looking for a place called Roswell, but became woefully lost as it was her first solo mission."*

"In her defence though, Roswell and Falkland have remarkably similar landscapes," Larry chimed in. *"We probably would have made the same error while looking for her, if not for the radio chatter that led us to your town."*

And with that, Mary and Georgio left Larry behind as they went to explore the rest of the ship. Immediately on the other side of the sliding door was a large white room, about the size of Mary's third grade classroom. There were two other doors on either side of the room, a counter that ran along one wall, and three sets of surprisingly Earth-like tables and chairs, which Mary supposed made sense; the aliens stood upright and had two legs just like humans, of course they had chairs! Several unfamiliar plants hung from the ceiling in small translucent containers. It appeared to be a lunchroom of sorts. Because the technology was not of Earth, Mary had to use her imagination to figure things out, but her best guess was that the large device on the counter was a drink dispenser. She watched as another alien walked up to the large refrigerator-sized contraption in the corner and pressed several buttons. The alien appeared to grow frustrated as the buttons did not elicit the response from the machine that it was hoping for.

"This is the ship's break room," Georgio explained. *"While everyone in the crew has a kitchen in their living quarters, the break room is here for when someone wants a quick snack. Although, it could use some upgrades."*

The frustrated alien extended its long skinny hand and slapped the side of the machine, causing the centre of the machine to pop open, revealing a package of something that was extended outwardly on a tray. *Ah, it's a vending machine,* Mary realized.

"Let me show you to your quarters," Georgio offered while leading Mary down another hallway.

"How many live on this ship?" Mary asked.

"Only ten Photoneons live on this craft. Photoneon is the name of our people, as I imagine you were curious about. We will be linking up with others soon though, where there will be hundreds of us!" Sensing that Mary had more questions due to her own raised eyebrows, Georgio continued. *"Since our people's ships are so small, we meet up frequently to share resources and to have large social gatherings. We were on our way to a special convention before we picked you up."*

"Does that mean I will get to go to it too?"

"It does. This one will be less fun than some of our other gatherings though. It will be more formal, as we need to discuss some pertinent news. You do not need to worry about that though, Larry and I will help you to prepare."

"Thank you," Mary replied. She wasn't often invited to things, so her inclusion felt special.

Georgio paused in front of another door. *"These are your quarters,"* he announced as the door began to slide open. Mary braced herself. She was going to have her very own bedroom on a spaceship! Surely this would be an exciting experience. The door slid open only to reveal... almost nothing. The walls, floor, and ceiling were all blindingly white and except for a small bed with a single blanket on it, the room was entirely bare. *"Are you disappointed?"* Georgio asked as he and Mary stepped into the room.

"No, not exactly... I am grateful to be here and to have my own room. I guess I'm just confused. It's so... empty?" Mary stared at the empty white walls. "And there are no windows."

"I'm sorry, I should explain things," Georgio offered. *"May I take your hand?"* Mary reached out and placed her hand in Georgio's; his long metallic fingers wrapped around Mary's soft skin as he placed her palm against the bedroom wall. Mary noticed that his hand was quite warm, not at all cool like a lizard as this species' scales indicated they may be. *"Visualize exactly how you would like the room to look."*

Closing her eyes as tightly as she could, Mary tried to imagine a fancy house from one of her mother's magazines. All of a sudden, a chandelier blipped into existence in the middle of the otherwise empty room. *"Keep focusing,"* Georgio offered.

Next, a pile of lush blankets appeared, neatly folded on top of the formerly sparse bed, followed by a sudden onslaught of no fewer than one hundred boxes of chocolate.

"You have a very powerful imagination," Georgio communicated, while nudging at a box of chocolate with his long foot. *"Is this how your people decorate their bedrooms on Earth?"*

"Not exactly," Mary replied with a mouthful of chocolate. She couldn't remember the last time she'd had candy, and after the commotion of the previous day, she was extremely hungry. "Can I really create *anything* in here?" she asked while using her finger to pick a piece of sticky nougat out of a molar.

"Absolutely anything, and anywhere," Georgio replied. *"Larry, for example, likes to pretend he lives underwater."*

"Wow," Mary mumbled with a mouthful of chocolate, already on her third piece.

"Wow indeed! It is quite spectacular. I prefer something simpler though," Georgio confessed. *"I like to pretend that I live in a small home in the forest back on our home world of Photonon."* In that moment, something about Georgio's eyes made Mary realize that there was something melancholic about him.

"Could you tell me more about your home world?" Mary asked.

"Certainly. Let's talk more tomorrow though, you should get some rest now," Georgio offered as he began to leave. *"The washroom*

is around the corner." He gestured to another concealed sliding door off to the side of the bedroom.

Once Georgio left, Mary found that the chandelier and other embellishments began to fade if she stopped thinking about them. Before long, the room was once again completely bare. Mary walked around the room, running her hands along the exceedingly clean white walls. Back at home, she would have gotten yelled at for touching the walls, even though the wallpaper was already peeling. Something to do with manners, or whatever. It felt ironic, especially considering the messes that her mother and stepfather would leave around the house. Mary sat on the bare white bed and sighed. Being onboard a real live alien spacecraft, and with her very own bedroom, was a dream come true. However, she couldn't shake the feeling that something was wrong.

Mary closed her eyes and focused as hard as she could and imagined her bedroom back on Earth. She imagined the peeling wallpaper, the dirty carpet, and even the dust on the nightstand. And just like that, it was as if she was back at home. She hopped up off of the bed, and went over to the windowsill where she found an exact replica of the cardboard paper towel tube that she and her little brother Georgie would use as a telescope. She held the fragile paper tube in her hands and sighed. For all of the wonder that she was surrounded by, Mary wanted nothing more than for Georgie to be here in the spaceship with her. She hoped that he was okay, and that she would be back home with him soon.

Chapter Four

Sunday, July 7th (1963)

The sun had only just begun to rise and yet Penticton's Main Street was already alive with the sounds of delivery trucks and squabbling gulls. After another late night, the birds and brakes became a terrible blend of migraine-inducing screeches that George could no longer bear. His head was pounding so hard that it felt like his brain was going to start oozing from his ears. Still rubbing the grit from his eyes, George rolled out of bed and slammed the single-paned window shut as quickly as he could.

Summers in Penticton were notoriously hot and George wasn't paid quite enough to be able to afford an air conditioner, which meant that he needed to sleep with the windows open. Living on Main Street wasn't all bad though; it was walking distance to the beach and orchards. Plus, the tree fruit was free as long as the farmers weren't around.

Just as George began to climb back into bed, the alarm clock went off with such ferocity it vibrated right off of the nightstand and crashed on to the hardwood floor. George closed his eyes and sighed while making a silent promise to himself to not stay out so late the next time he needed to wake up early. And to finally buy ear plugs.

The alarm clock had been set for the hellishly early hour of 5:00AM, since George needed to drive all the way to Vernon in order to be there in time for visiting hours at the Dellview Hospital, before going to Falkland for the night. Dellview was an institution for the mentally unwell, as polite people would say. Most people weren't polite though, and it was more commonly known as the loony bin, nuthatch, or cuckoo's nest. And in George's case, it was also where his mother lived.

***

After a less-than-hearty breakfast of orange juice and a stack of Ritz Crackers, George rushed downstairs and towards his old Chevy that was parked off of the street. He tossed his overnight bag on the floor of the passenger's seat, taking care not to crush the cardboard tubes that were on the seat itself. The tubes contained several star charts that George had printed at work the day before, and while he didn't think he would get fired if the researchers knew why he was printing the maps at work in the first place, he didn't want to risk it. At best, he would need to explain the entire story of how his sister went missing and his coworkers would give him their sympathies. George would sooner be fired than have everyone at work feel sorry for him.

He winced as he grabbed the steering wheel; the interior had already gotten warm thanks to the intense Okanagan sun. In a moment of panic, George shifted the truck back into park and scrambled to unroll the star charts from the cardboard tubes they were stored in. The charts were printed on transparency paper – the heat could cause them to melt! George frantically unrolled them and breathed a huge sigh of relief when he discovered that they were fine and had not melted together. It was one thing to use the printers without permission, it would be a whole other issue to break into the observatory on a weekend to reprint the maps. Thankfully, that wouldn't be necessary.

George rolled down the windows, put on his sunglasses, and sped down Main Street towards the Trans Canada Highway. He would need to make one stop along the way – his mother would be furious if he forgot to bring her a stack of magazines – but other than that it would be a straight drive to Dellview.

Early morning dog walkers scowled as George's dusty old truck rumbled past them, but he didn't care. He already had enough on his mind. Even though he visited his mother, Margaret, weekly, George always found their visits to be extremely stressful. Simply put, George and his mother had a complicated history.

George would never forget the night that he spent staring out of his bedroom window, waiting for Mary to come home. How he ran towards his mom as fast as his little feet would take him when he spotted her, out of breath and stumbling through the backyard and back to their house.

"Did you see the aliens, Mommy?" the then four-year-old George asked Margaret.

"I did, Georgie, I did. They took Mary with them." Margaret tried her best to catch her breath as she knelt down and gave George the biggest hug he had ever gotten up until then, and hadn't experienced since. Once the sun had risen and Margaret had managed to straighten herself out, she went to the police station with George in tow. She presumed that if anyone would be able to help her get her daughter back, the officers who witnessed the entire ordeal would. Once at the station though, the very police officers that had witnessed Mary leave with the aliens acted like the incident never happened. In fact, they implied that Margaret was a liar, or worse, "unwell." Even as a toddler, George thought the entire incident was bizarre.

"Are you alright, Ma'am?" the first officer asked.

"Cut the nonsense, I know you were there last night!" Margaret pushed.

"Have you been drinking?" the second officer chimed in with fake concern. "Because what you're saying sounds like the ramblings of someone with a drinking problem..."

"Are you really pretending that last night didn't happen?" Margaret retorted, this time with a hint of nervousness. This was the first time George had ever heard his mom sound uneasy like that.

"My mommy doesn't lie!" George proclaimed.

"Hey kiddo, we're not saying your mom is a liar. We're just concerned that maybe she's had one too many pops. Or maybe she's feeling... under the weather. It can be exhausting being a single mother and, sometimes when we're tired, our brains make us see things that aren't there..." the first officer trailed off.

"No, you're... you're probably right," Margaret conceded. "Mommy?" George asked, confused, while pulling at the hem of his mother's linen shirt. His mom was never one to shy away from confrontation. This made him feel very uneasy.

"It's okay, Georgie. I had a late night. Mary is probably out camping. She'll... come home soon," Margaret said to the officers, rather than to George.

He would never forget the confusion he felt as he and his mother left the police station, or how his mother had turned as white as a ghost. The officers stopped by later that evening and seized several of Mary's belongings, including the ray gun which little Georgie had carefully hidden underneath his pillow. He wasn't sure what else they took, but he knew that they didn't have permission. After that, his mother became withdrawn. She no longer went out to meet friends or to get groceries. In fact, she barely left the house at all. As time went on, she became increasingly reliant on George for help, and for conversation. After the incident at the police station, he was one of the few people that she still spoke to. Everyone in Falkland thought she had lost her mind. Everyone, except for George.

The situation with Margaret deteriorated to its lowest around the time George was a teenager. A concerned citizen – or a busybody, as Margaret would call them – had contacted the police when they allegedly spotted Margaret sobbing during one of her rare solo trips to the grocery store. Margaret was always adamant to George that she hadn't broken down in the store that day, but as with Mary's disappearance, no one believed her. Without a spouse or any other mature family members to advocate for her, Margaret was sent to the Dellview Hospital, where she remained to this day.

Although he was technically placed under the guardianship of one of the local teachers, Susan Webb, George was able to stay at his family home and fend for himself until he finished high school and got his job as an assistant at the Dominion Radio Astrophysical Observatory. And now, here he was, two years out of high school and driving his old beat-up trunk to visit his mother at the Dellview Psychiatric Hospital just as he did every weekend.

Chapter Five

Wednesday, July 9th (1947) - Stardate 194707.09

After an indeterminate amount of time, Mary awoke to find that the bedroom had reverted back to its entirely blank state. This was a small relief, because Mary had dreamt that she was back camping by the river and she really didn't want to clean up the mess caused by the campfire.

Mary got out of bed and stretched as tall as her tiny frame could manage when her stomach let out the most ravenous grumble she had ever experienced. *"How can I be so hungry?"* she wondered out loud to herself. After all, Mary had visualized and eaten several cheeseburgers before bed. It was then that she realized that the imaginary food likely didn't have any calories when it was digested. This was probably all well and good for a dieting housewife, but not for a skinny nine-year-old who needed all the nutrition she could get. A sense of panic filled Mary as she realized she hadn't consumed any actual food since the leftover piece of Dominion Day cake two days prior. Suddenly, she felt as if she might faint. Mary ran around, frantically running her hand along the bedroom's blank walls. Where the heck was the sliding door to the kitchen? *"Oh no,"* Mary thought, *"I'm going to be the first human to die in space. And of starvation! Not even of somethin' neat like fighting off a space monster..."*

Just then, Larry and Georgio emerged from the sliding door that opened to the hallway. "I am so happy to see you!" Mary cried out while running towards the two lanky Photoneons. "Where is the kitchen?"

"It's right over there," Georgio explained, gesturing to what appeared to be one of the plain white walls. Mary stood in her place, confused.

"Oh no. I don't think she can see the labels," Larry communicated to Georgio.

"Mary, this may be a complicated question for you but..." Georgio trailed off, which was odd for someone communicating telepathically. *"How many photoreceptors are in the human eye?"*

"How many whatchas?" Mary responded, confused. "We haven't started learning about body parts in class."

"How many colours can you see?" Larry asked.

"Um... let me count. Red, blue, yellow, purple, orange, green... violet... pink... indigo... but that might just be blue. Do you want all of the different kinds of blue?" Mary asked, even more confused.

"I have an idea," Larry announced telepathically before leaving the room and returning with two pens, which he and Larry used to label all of the doors for Mary. When they were

finished, Mary was astounded to realize that her bedroom not only had its own bathroom and kitchen, but also extensive closet space. The closet space confused Mary, since the aliens didn't seem to wear any clothes. She added this to her long list of questions to ask later.

"This is your kitchen," Georgio explained. *"I am exceedingly sorry that you didn't have access during the past several hours. Here, let us show you how everything works."* As with the rest of the bedroom, the entire kitchen was empty, except for two white cubes on the counter, and a sink. The sink surprised Mary because it looked like something from Earth. She wasn't sure why she kept expecting everything on the ship to look so… alien. After all, the Photoneons clearly weren't too different than her. Sure, they had blue scales, stood roughly two feet taller that regular grown-ups, and didn't appear to be wearing clothes, but their mannerisms made them feel much more relatable than radio shows had led Mary to imagine.

"This first box is your food printer," Georgio said, gesturing to the first of the two cubes with his long sinewy hands. *"It contains several key ingredients which it then mixes together into a variety of foods. Just press one of the buttons on the side and it will make that food!"* Mary stared at the blank cube, before Larry and Georgio knowingly picked up the pens again and used them to draw buttons on the cube that Mary's eyes could see. It was clear that Georgio was the better artist of the two.

"The second box is the refrigerator, in case you have leftovers," Georgio continued, as Larry drew a picture on it that seemed

to resemble an alien snowman. While Mary was thankful to be able to see the buttons, the kitchen looked even less science fiction-y now that there were cartoon sketches drawn on everything. *"Try it out,"* Georgio offered excitedly. Unsure of what any of their drawings were supposed to be, Mary reached for the button that appeared to have a plate of spaghetti on it.

"That's a brave choice," Larry communicated with an uneasy tone.

Mary lifted her finger and held it above another symbol, which looked more like a stack of pancakes. Georgio nodded as if to imply that this would be a safer choice, so Mary held her breath and pressed the button. She was so hungry that she would eat whatever the machine printed for her, so she sincerely hoped it would be delicious and not a plate of worms. The machine hummed for a moment, and then stopped.

Ding!

The front of the white cube opened up, revealing… a stack of pancakes! Including syrup! Mary was so relieved. She immediately grabbed the fork Larry held out and began eating as quickly as she could.

"This machine has been programmed to be able to make several popular Earth dishes for you," Georgio explained while Mary scarfed down the pancakes. *"When you're done, please put the dishes back in the machine to be reconstituted—"*

"Wait, what does the other button make?" Mary interrupted, gesturing at the button that Larry had referred to as a brave choice.

"That's spaghetti," Georgio explained, *"Larry hates it because it reminds him of worms."*

***

After finishing three plates of pancakes, and with reassurance from Larry and Georgio that it was in fact real food and that she would stay full this time, Mary was taken on a tour of the spaceship. This time Georgio needed to work his shift at the ship's helm running all of the control panels, so she was paired off with Larry. At first glance, the two beings looked remarkably similar, so Mary tried her best to notice the differences between them so that she would never get them mixed up. The tour wasn't that exciting since all of the rooms looked nearly identical, so she found herself staring up at Larry for most of it.

"Why do you keep examining me?" Larry asked after several minutes.

"I want to know what makes you different, so I don't get you mixed up with Georgio," Mary admitted.

"I wouldn't mind being mixed up with Georgio," Larry replied with an honesty that Mary wasn't used to. *"He's my best friend. Also, he's shorter, which I think would be nice."*

"That's a really interesting answer," Mary replied. "Humans don't like being short."

"Why not?" Larry asked, perplexed.

"I'm not sure," Mary replied. "I think maybe they prefer to be tall because the world is big and scary."

"On a spaceship, being short means that you have more room! If you are tall, living aboard a spaceship can feel claustrophobic."

"Do you get claustrophobic?" Mary asked.

"Sometimes," Larry replied, *"but thankfully there is lots of room to stretch out and to be more comfortable when my people's ships link up for parties and conferences."*

"I bet those are lots of fun."

"They are. It can be lonely on such a small ship, but when we all get together, it is like no time has passed at all," Larry explained while gesturing to another empty white room that they were walking by. *"That's our classroom. There are three children on this ship, so this is where they go to learn."*

Mary lit up. "Will I get to meet them?"

"If you would like, I am sure they could learn a lot from you," Larry replied enthusiastically.

"I would like that a lot," Mary answered earnestly. She wasn't expecting to meet other children on this adventure and was happy to possibly play with someone other than the usual schoolyard bullies.

One thing in particular that stood out to her was just how quiet the ship was. Other than a slight electronic buzz that reverberated through the walls, the ship was silent. It made sense to Mary, on account of the aliens communicating with telepathy — of course there wouldn't be any sounds of idle chitchat if everyone is communicating through their thoughts. The silence was concerning to Mary, though. She thought about her portable radio left behind on Earth. Even during the darkest and scariest of times, Mary always had music and the voices on the radio to comfort her. On a silent ship, she wasn't sure what she would do if she were to become sad and there was no one around to talk to. She was very much looking forward to meeting the other children on the ship. Suddenly, Mary heard the welcome sounds of chatter.

"Chit-chit-chit shhhhhhriek!"

"Rica rica chit chit."

"Click, click... Womp."

And then, with only a few seconds of warning, three small alien children excitedly ran past Mary and Larry and into the classroom. The alien children were shorter than Mary, which surprised her. They were also much bluer than Mary, which didn't surprise her. The children were much chubbier than their adult counterparts. In a way, they were like human toddlers. Like Georgie.

"I thought that your people didn't speak to each other?" Mary asked.

"Telepathy is a skill that must be learned. Ray, for example, was only just learning how to use her telepathy. These children haven't even begun their training, so they speak quite loudly. And walk loudly, and sit loudly..." Larry stared at the three rambunctious students running around the classroom. One was throwing a ball against the classroom wall. Mary noticed an exhaustion in his eyes that she hadn't previously picked up on. *"Unfortunately, they won't be able to communicate with you just yet,"* Larry continued, *"However, you are encouraged to go and play with them—"*

Before he could finish his sentence, Mary was already in the classroom and introducing herself to the other kids. Larry smiled internally as he stood back and watched his species' children eagerly introduce themselves to Mary. It made him happy to see that while they didn't speak the same verbal language, the children all seemed to share the universal understanding of what it meant to play. Larry still needed to tell Mary some very important things before the big conference tomorrow, but he decided that after everything she had been through, she deserved to have fun first.

Chapter Six

Sunday, July 7th (1963)

With a stack of news and fashion magazines held under his increasingly sweaty arm, George paced awkwardly at the doorway of the Dellview Hospital. No matter how hard he tried, he would always hum and haw for several minutes before being able to bring himself to actually go inside.

The hospital was located on the outer edges of the city, since the decision makers at city hall thought it would be best to build the hospital away from the general population. George knew that well-to-do members of society didn't want to think about what went on in facilities like that, and they definitely wouldn't have tolerated it being built next to a mall or a department store. Imagine trying to shop at Eaton's while knowing that there were institutionalized people living across the street? That would have been true lunacy! After all, no decent people would choose to go insane, which meant that everyone at Dellview had clearly deserved to be pushed aside to the outer limits of the city. Out of sight, out of mind. Although the area was surrounded by orchards, it was difficult to appreciate the beauty around the hospital when you knew what the people inside of the hospital were being subjected to. George had grown used to the long drive here, but walking through the front door was always difficult. He could sense that the receptionist was watching him from the other side of the glass door and didn't want her to think that he was anxious or scared, but just couldn't bring himself to enter the facility right away because of the fear that one day he would visit his mother and not be allowed to leave.

"No one wants their loved ones to end up in a place like this, but hey, what can you do sometimes?" an older woman offered sympathetically while pushing a wheelchair along the sidewalk and towards the doorway that George was standing in.

"Oh! I'm so sorry — here, let me get the door for you," George said while opening the door for the woman and helping to pull the wheelchair through the door. He was so caught up in helping with the chair that he didn't realize he had finally walked through the door.

"Thank you for your help," the paunchy woman replied. "I didn't want to make any assumptions, you just looked like you could use some friendly words. I'm Tammy, one of the nurses here."

"It's nice to meet you, I'm George," George said while shaking the nurse's hand.

"Oh! You must be Margaret's boy!" Tammy replied. George tried his best to take the nurse's words at face value and to not make any assumptions. He needed to remember that not everyone was judging him and no one was going to assume he was insane because his mother was locked up.

"Yeah, I'm out here every week to see my mom... she's expecting me, so..." George began to mumble as he became increasingly uncomfortable with the small talk about his mother.

"I just started here a week ago, but I heard your mom used to think she was abducted by aliens or something. That must have been really difficult for you, but sending her here was the right decision," Tammy rambled on. George's gut instinct was correct; this person was a judgmental busybody.

"It wasn't that she was abducted... It was my sister... Anyway..." George could feel his chest tighten. He hated speaking to strangers about his sister. It wasn't their bloody business. "I also wasn't the one that put my mom in here." George took a deep breath and chose to walk away from the nurse mid sentence. Who cared what she thought of him, anyway.

***

"Did you meet that new nurse, Tammy?" Margaret asked before clearing her throat and lighting a fresh cigarette. The smell of burning tobacco and who-knows-what-else wafted around her like a toxic aura.

"Yeah, she's quite... talkative," George replied while futilely trying to move his chair so he wouldn't be caught in the cloud of tar and nicotine. Since being admitted to Dellview, Margaret had taken to chain smoking. At one point, George had tried to convince her to stop because he hated smelling like cigarettes every time he left the hospital, but she told him it was the only thing she could do to occupy her time and he should either start smoking too or learn to mind his own business. According to her, he should just run around after each visit to shake off the smell. George of course knew that idea was nonsense, but didn't have the energy to argue with her anymore.

"Tammy is a complete ninny," Margaret said, enunciating each word's syllables as clearly as she could. It was obvious that she did not want George to disagree with the ninniness of the nurse.

George struggled to think of anything to say to his mother. He couldn't exactly ask if she had gone anywhere new lately, had any visitors, or even had anything decent for dinner. She wasn't allowed to leave the hospital, had no friends, and the food here was horrid. The magazines he brought with him each visit were Margaret's sole form of entertainment.

"Ah. It looks like that princess is finally getting married," George said with as much enthusiasm as he could muster as he passed Margaret the magazines that he brought. It was then that he noticed the bruises on his mother's thin, sun-spotted arms. "Mom. What the hell are those from?" George asked, immediately dropping the forced sweetness in his voice.

"These things? Pfft, who knows," Margaret replied, holding up her arm as if she was inspecting the bruises for the first time. "They just happen sometimes. The bed is like concrete, you know that. The bruises are probably from that."

"On your wrists though?" George asked, sensing his mother wasn't being forthcoming.

"Hey, stranger things have happened," Margaret replied nonchalantly, before letting out a short raspy laugh when she realized the dark irony of her statement.

"Mom..."

"Don't *mom* me, Georgie. It's probably nothing. Besides, it's not like either of us could do anything about it if it *was* something."

Although George knew she was deflecting, his mom was right. There wasn't anything either of them could do to get her out of here. He had pushed to become her caregiver several times over the years, but because he was her child, the nurses said he wasn't a reliable judge of his mother's character. The judge that had signed her commitment papers wouldn't even answer any of his calls. Once, after a particularly late night, George was considering contacting the police from Falkland that he knew were responsible for his mother's commitment, but once he sobered up, he realized he could never find Mary if he was also institutionalized. There was something fishy happening at the Dellview Hospital, but he knew he wouldn't be the one to get to the bottom of it. Maybe one day someone else would, but by then it would be too late for people receiving forced treatment like his mother was.

"Let's change the topic, shall we?" Margaret prompted. "How are you?"

"I'm okay, work's going well," George replied. "I am really learning a lot from being around those scientists."

Margaret went silent. Sometimes she was eager to hear about his job, while other times it would upset her. George knew that his mother understood why he was pursuing a career in astronomy in the first place, but sometimes the mention of his job would cause her to become despondent. Although they had a silent agreement to never use Mary's name while Margaret was in the facility, sometimes even the mere reminder of her existence was enough to push Margaret into a dark place. George refused to give up though.

"I wish you'd forget about *her*." The way that Margaret spat out that sentence, it was as if the word itself had a bitter flavour. "I'm aware of what day tomorrow is, Georgie."

"I assumed so," George replied. "It's been sixteen years… Don't you want to say anything about her?"

"There's nothing left to say." Margaret's gaze began to shift away from George and off into some unknown distant place.

George was so desperate to hear Margaret say Mary's name, to reminisce with his mom about literally any moment from his childhood before his sister went missing, but he doubted that would ever happen. He could feel the water welling up behind his eyes; thankfully, that was something he could blame on the cigarette smoke that had now filled Margaret's room.

"I should get going, it's getting hard to breathe in here," George said as he leaned in to give his mother a hug. "I'll see you next week."

"If you see Tammy on your way out, tell her I think she's a nincompoop," Margaret said mid-embrace.

"Okay, Mom," George replied.

Chapter Seven

Thursday, July 10th (1947) – Stardate 194707.10

After playing with the rambunctious group of alien toddlers, Mary slept exceptionally well. Instead of imagining that she was back in her old room, this time Mary decided to picture a much more comfortable bed: one made of cotton candy and clouds. Mary was a very literal thinker and was the most content when she understood how things around her worked. Once she understood that the imagination controls in the ship's living quarters were a hybrid technology of a brain scanner and augmented reality (and after Larry had explained the definitions of each of those new words), Mary felt as if she had permission from herself to dream big, figuratively and literally. Everything she imagined was just that, imaginary. She wasn't betraying her family on Earth by sleeping comfortably in space. As Mary began to wake up and the fluffy sugar-based mattress began to fade, she heard a knock at the door. "Come in!" she called out, taking a bite of the imaginary cotton candy before it fully faded away.

When the door to Mary's bedroom slid open, she was not expecting to see Larry and Georgio standing there in uncharacteristically fancy clothes. Or rather, any clothes. Mary had always wondered if they were always naked, and now she supposed, she had her answer.

"What are you wearing?" Mary said with a hint of amusement in her voice.

"This is the formal attire that we are forced to wear for conferences," Georgio answered as Larry awkwardly fidgeted with something on the end of his long, flowing sleeves. Except for the rainbow-bejeweled trims along the edges of the robe, the rest of the material was silver and, perhaps most unexpectedly, slightly wrinkled, as if they had been hanging in a closet for quite some time. Despite the humour of the situation, Mary thought that they robes looked very pretty and that Larry and Georgio would make excellent models for her mom's favourite magazine, *Chatelaine.*

"We try not to be rude in front of guests, but Mary, we need to be honest with you," Larry said. *"We hate wearing these robes. They are itchy and ugly and serve very little practical purpose."*

Sensing Mary would inevitably have a follow-up question, Georgio picked up where Larry left off. *"The robes are ceremonial. They're one of the few remaining traditions that we continue from our home planet. But, as Larry mentioned, they are exceedingly itchy."*

"I like the jewels," Mary offered.

"Thank you," Larry and Georgio both replied.

No longer able to contain herself, Mary asked the question that she had had since she met Ray back on Earth. "Why don't you wear spacesuits?" she blurted out.

"The ship is temperature controlled," Georgio replied.

"And it was summer on Earth when Ray landed," Larry expanded, gesturing with a single long finger in order to empathize his point.

Mary only nodded as she came to terms with the fact that she was apparently living on a nudist spaceship.

"Do I need to dress up too?" Mary asked while looking down at her tattered blue dress. She hadn't changed her clothes in a few days now, and was hoping for a chance to wear one of the fancy robes like her two blue friends.

"You are encouraged to wear one, if you would like," Georgio replied. *"Our people have never met a human before, so having you wear one of our traditional outfits might make them feel less alarmed."*

Mary had not considered the idea that she herself might be frightening to someone. She thought of her scaleless face, her head full of hair, and her stubby human fingers... While she always considered herself to be an okay-looking person back on Earth, it was understandable that these features might be shocking to someone else. After all, on this ship, Mary was the alien.

***

Several hours later, and now in her own long flowing bejeweled robe, Mary was peering through the ship's lone window in the control centre. Since their journey from Earth, the ship had traveled to a particularly remote part of space. One might assume that all of space was remote, but this spot was even more remote than the most remote spot that an Earth kid like Mary could imagine.

While space was typically aglow with all sorts of distant stars and planets regardless of where you were, this spot was mostly black. According to Georgio, they were in a region of space known only as the Void. They were there because it was the safest part of space; there would be no risk of an asteroid or anything else hitting any of the ships. Avoiding asteroids was of utmost importance to the Photoneon race. Mary felt as if she wasn't being told the entire story, but was assured that she would be caught up on everything once the conference started. In the meantime, she was told to wait and watch the arrival of the ships while Larry and Georgio worked on some final preparations.

From where the ship was parked, the closest stars appeared smaller than the smallest grains of sand. They were so distant in fact that Mary wasn't sure if she could actually see them, or if her brain was simply placing imaginary stars outside because Mary's subconscious couldn't fathom the idea of an entirely empty sky. As Mary stared out at the extremely distant stars, it started to appear as if they were growing closer. She rubbed her eyes thinking that the strain of staring out at the black nothingness must be causing her to imagine things.

But then she was certain – the lights were growing closer at an accelerating rate! Within a matter of moments dozens of other spaceships, all varying sizes and colours, were beginning to gather. Mary was surprised that not all of them were silver like the saucer that she was on: some were green, some were pink, heck, one ship was painted rainbow! Although on closer inspection, it appeared to be coated in various squiggles and letters, as if someone had doodled all over it like an old train car. Once all of the ships had arrived, they began to form a circle.

Suddenly, a loud "THWUCK" sound reverberated through the ship as a large tube unfolded from a concealed panel on the side of every ship. The tubes connected in the middle of the circle of ships to form vast corridors, linking every ship together. From Mary's vantage point, it was a beautiful sight. It was incredible to see so many ships coordinate with one another like that. She imagined that from above, or below – those sorts of directions didn't matter too much in space – the conjoined ships must look like a constellation of a dandelion.

After the connection process was complete, both Larry and Georgio returned to the control centre. *"Before the conference begins, there is someone important that you need to speak to,"* Georgio communicated. There was a somber look to his eyes that made Mary nervous.

"Is everything okay? Am I in trouble?" Mary asked anxiously.

"Why would you be in trouble? You haven't done anything wrong," Larry assured her. *"There are, however, certain things you should know before the festivities begin."*

And so, Mary pushed any worries she had about being in trouble deep down into the bottom of her stomach, and followed Larry and Georgio into the newly-formed corridor linking all of the ships together. Mary hadn't noticed during the initial linking, but the left and right sides of the hall were entirely transparent. The view was absolutely magnificent. She wasn't the best with distance and measurements, but guessed it was roughly one kilometre from her spaceship to the centre of the connected corridor. Whether she looked left or right, there was an uninterrupted view of all of the multi-coloured spacecrafts. It was the prettiest walk that she had ever gone on. Except for the gentle sounds of their foot steps and the idle buzz from the ship's electronics that Mary had already grown used to, Mary once again noticed how quiet the ship was. She wished that there was music playing through the hallway, maybe something by Frank Sinatra. She started to hum *When Sleepy Stars Begin to Fall.*

"Doo doo doo, doo dooooo..."

"What are you doing?" Larry asked, coming to a standstill midway down the hallway.

"Oh! Humming, I guess," Mary replied shyly. She hadn't even realized she was doing it.

"I have heard about this," Georgio said. *"It's not something I have ever seen for myself though. This is truly fascinating. Why do you do it?"*

"I just like music is all." Mary shrugged.

"Could you teach us?" Georgio asked. While he wasn't able to connote much tone through telepathy alone, Mary could tell by the changes to his pupils that he was quite excited.

"Sure," Mary answered. "Put your lips—" Mary paused when she realized that neither Larry nor Georgio were going to be asked to be in a kissing booth anytime soon. "Um, put your mouth together, like this," she demonstrated, "then make a sound, as if you're going to speak, but have forgotten the words."

"But what sound should we make?" Larry asked.

"Do you have a favourite song?" Mary questioned.

"We don't have music on our planet," Larry answered in a matter-of-fact way that Mary found sad.

"No music?" Mary paused while thinking of a reply that wouldn't hurt either of the alien's feelings. "That's okay, I will teach you a song!"

With that, Mary was suddenly watching both Larry and Georgio attempt to hum along to *Hot Crossed Buns.* Their pitch wasn't great, but it looked as if they were enjoying themselves which made Mary happy. In the distance she spotted several other extraterrestrials watching in amusement from their ships' portions of the windowed corridor. Mary was not sure if they would be more or less confused if they could have also heard the impromptu music lesson.

When Mary and the duo of newly-minted songbirds eventually made their way to the end of the hall and into the small reception area, several of their long-distance audience members gathered around to find out what they had been doing. *"We were humming!"* Larry proclaimed. *"Our new crew member, Mary, taught us!"*

Several of the onlookers, all dressed in identical bejeweled robes, peered down at Mary and gasped.

"She is a human," Georgio answered, more seriously. *"We rescued her when we were looking for Ray."*

"Hi," Mary replied awkwardly with a single wave as she peered up at the group of curious beings.

"Despite her scary appearance of smooth skin and chubby fingers, she is not dangerous," Larry elaborated. Mary was unsure that she was supposed to receive that telepathic message.

"Can... this being... can she teach us to hum too?" One of the onlookers asked, its pupils flickering with excitement. Several others nodded along, indicating their elation at this idea.

"Sure, if you would like?" Mary answered, not used to being the centre of attention. She felt particularly short in this moment as she was being increasingly surrounded by all of these seven-foot-tall beings.

"We have a stop to make first," Georgio replied, while placing his hand on Mary's shoulder. *"But afterwards, if she would like to teach you, then we can all hum. Come though, Mary, there is some-one you need to meet,"* he continued while escorting her past the others.

"Where are you going?" One of the snoopier crowd members communicated.

"Are you taking her to meet the Cleric?" An even snoopier individual asked as Mary was led out of the gathering area and down a hall towards another ship.

***

"Before you go in, there is something you should know," Georgio explained to Mary while leaning down to straighten out the collar on her robe, then fixing both Larry's and his own. *"The person behind this door is the oldest living member of our species. She has remained almost entirely in isolation since moving onto her ship, and only makes brief excursions from her room—"*

"It's okay, I'm good with old people," Mary interrupted while fidgeting with the sleeves on her robe. She hoped that the loose string that she noticed was there when they gave her the robe, and that she hadn't already made a snag in the fancy article of clothing...

"She is expecting you, but we need to ask you to be careful with her. Some people find her way of communicating to be... outdated. But we rely on her for much. The Cleric is responsible for all of the big decisions that impact our people," Georgio continued.

"Big decisions, like what?" Mary asked, arching her eyebrow. It was odd that her two alien compatriots were acting so vaguely.

"She will explain everything," Larry answered as the sliding door to the Cleric's room opened, causing both he and Georgio to stand at attention.

"Thank you, congregates," the unseen voice of the Cleric communicated. *"You may send her in."*

Chapter Eight

Sunday, July 7th (1963)

"You know, I really wish you'd visit more often," Susan Webb whined from the living room as George stood in the kitchen, slowly stirring a dollop of honey into her cup of tea. Red Rose was Susan's favourite. George used to enjoy a good cup of tea as well, but after the years of listening to Susan's metal spoon ting against the walls of the ceramic mug – always the same one, too – he grew to hate it. Perhaps 'hate' was too strong of a word. He had grown annoyed with tea. The way Susan talked his ear off while he boiled her water, the way she went on and on about how much he reminded her of his late father as she stirred honey into her cup, and the awful sipping sound that Susan made as she drank it. Yessiree, tea was extremely annoying.

"Here you go," George said, as politely as he could, as he sat down on her plastic-covered floral couch. *At least it's just two nights,* George thought as one of Susan's many cats hopped on his lap and proceeded to stick its butt far too close to George's face. At one point, George made an effort to learn each of their names, but over the years, they all started to blend together. Fluffy, Foo-Foo, Mr. Kits, Mr. Fluffy, and at one time, two sibling kittens she had called Mary and Georgie before the human George convinced her to name them absolutely anything else. He tried his best to pet the current cat with the back of his hand so that the beast's fur wouldn't stick to his palm and eventually get into his eyes. George liked cats, he really did, but he was horribly allergic to them. Allergies, and the weird complicated history that Susan had with the Schmidt family, made these annual visits extremely uncomfortable.

It wasn't easy for him to admit that he didn't enjoy these visits; after all, Susan had stepped up and became his legal guardian when Margaret was committed. He felt that he owed her his loyalty for saving him from a life in the foster system. But as George had grown up, and listened to more and more of Susan's stories, it was clear that she had no business adopting a child. Especially the child of a man she may have been engaged to twenty years prior. Between his mother and Susan, George knew he'd never get the entire true story. Frankly though, he no longer cared. The only thing that was positive about their lunches together was that it used to give George something to talk about when he'd visited his mother in Dellview. Eventually though, he felt like he was adding too much negativity into the world by having such heated gossip sessions with his mother, so he stopped telling her when he had visited Susan. And then, even more eventually, he only stopped by to see Susan when he made his annual trip to Falkland on the anniversary of Mary's disappearance.

"It's so interesting to me that you visit Falkland each year on the day your sister vanished," Susan said before taking a loud sip of her drink. George closed his eyes, lest he roll them impolitely, as he anticipated the exact words that would come out of her mouth next. "Because if someone close to me was brutally eaten by bears or whatever happened, I would want to stay far away from the town on that day of all days."

"I know. You tell me that every year..." George trailed off as the orange cat finally hopped down to the floor.

"I miss Mary so much! She was one of my star pupils. If anyone misses Mary as much as you, it's probably me," Susan continued. "But I just can't imagine reliving it every year by going out to look for her. I don't know what you're hoping to find. There'd be nothing left of her at this point you know, Georgie."

"What can I say, I guess I'm just nostalgic," George replied, staring distantly out of the living room window. It was always odd to be back in Falkland. Nothing much ever seemed to change. Not even the state of Susan's flower garden, which was always immaculate. Despite her growing age, she always managed to keep everything perfect, almost obsessively so.

"Douglas was like that too, always thinking of the past... it was quite romantic, in a sense. I really loved that part of him," Susan spoke wistfully as she fidgeted with the handle of the tea cup.

"Susan..." George groaned.

"I'm sorry, *your father* was always like that too," Susan corrected herself. "Did I ever tell you about how back in his military days, he would—"

No longer able to tolerate the rambling stories where she would compare him to his father, George decided to do something that he had never done before. He told her the truth. "It makes me extremely uncomfortable to hear my late father's possible fiancée, probable obsessive admirer, compare me to him," George interrupted.

"Georgie!" Susan exclaimed.

"I appreciate that you were there for me when Mom was sent away, but I have been listening to the same inappropriate stories for a decade and they need to stop," George pressed.

"Okay, okay, I just—"

"No, let me speak. I don't care about what happened between you, my father, and my mother. I appreciate you and everything you've done, but this has gotten to be too weird. I want to keep both you and my mother in my life, but you both need to grow up." It felt weird for George to say these words to a fully grown adult, let alone someone on the cusp of becoming a senior citizen.

"I'm sorry," Susan replied as she set her tea down on top of a singular stain on the coffee table; she had completed this gesture identically so many times before that it was as if the table had a built-in coaster.

"It's okay," George said as he stood up. Noticing Susan's large sad eyes, he leaned in and gave her a hug. "I forgive you." As he ended the hug and walked towards the door he turned back, unable to resist adding two more points: "Also, Mary wasn't eaten by a bear, and aliens are real." The shocked look on his former guardian's face made him realize that he probably wasn't going to be welcome back for dinner. Oh well, that would give George an extra day to spend on his other plans.

Chapter Nine

Thursday, July 10th (1947) – Stardate 194707.10

Although the door in front of her was open, Mary chose to remain in the hallway for a moment longer. Something about the unseen voice had made her deeply uncomfortable. She wasn't sure if it was the darkness of the room ahead, or the voice itself, but a chill fell over Mary, from the top of her brunette head all of the way down to her toes. She turned back, looking for words of comfort from either Larry or Georgio, but they remained silent. It was clear that they had a great reverence for the person in this room, and possibly a little fear. Mary mustered up all of her bravery and stepped into the dark room. She realized that she had been holding her breath and inhaled deeply. The room had a slightly stale smell, as if the person inside hadn't gotten any fresh air in a very long time.

"Hi, I'm... I'm Mary," Mary offered as she peered through the dark room. As her eyes adjusted to the darkness, her gaze eventually fell on a small light that was shining next to what appeared to be a bed.

"Yes, come in," the owner of the earlier unseen voice called out.

Mary noticed that the voice belonged to an elderly individual that was laying in the bed. The Cleric.

"Take a seat," the Cleric said, gesturing towards a bedside chair as she slowly sat up in her bed. Although it was difficult to see much in the dark room, Mary observed that the Cleric's scales were much less blue and more grey than the rest of the Photoneons. The Cleric's eyes had a haze to them, something that Mary had also seen with elderly people back on Earth. This being was clearly very ancient.

"Wait." Mary noticed something else as she slid her chair closer to the Cleric's bed. "You can speak out loud?"

"Just the elderly and the babies, isn't that a hilarious irony? At a certain age, we lose our ability to communicate telepathically. I'd like to think it's because our heads get too full of knowledge," the Cleric replied with a small raspy laugh. And just like that, Mary's earlier fear began to fade away.

"Truth be told, I am extremely grateful to have you to speak with today. One can only make small talk with babies for so long before they start to feel like they've gone mad. I just wish you and I were meeting under better circumstances..." The Cleric cleared her throat and adjusted one of the buttons on the small translator device that she spoke into. "You are probably wondering why your two caretakers left you with me," the Cleric guessed. "Well, the truth is, they're scared of me. Perhaps 'scared' isn't the right word... Mary, is there someone on your planet that you are so desperate to make happy – that you are… so afraid to disappoint – that you simply choose to avoid them?"

Mary thought about her mother and her teacher. She paused for a moment before answering truthfully. "No."

"Oh," the Cleric replied. "That wasn't what I was expecting… Thank you for keeping this old lady on her toes!" The Cleric let out another raspy laugh. "Allow me to explain, then. I am the eldest member of our people, as well as the last survivor from the Last Migration. The people of Photonon hold their ancestors and history in great esteem. So, being the eldest means that everyone treats me with admiration and comes to me for important decisions. I used to enjoy being more social and hanging out with others on the ship but once the former eldest Photoneon died, the title of Cleric was given to me, and it came with all of the social pressure. Since then, I have spent most of my days hiding in my room. Another cruel irony is that I hid in here for so long, that now I am too old to go very far. Life is full of dark humour if you just look, Mary."

Mary paused for a moment, trying to think of the best question to ask the surprisingly verbose Cleric. "What was the Last Migration?"

"Ah yes, good question. That is also why you are here today," the Cleric continued. "There is a box in the corner of the room, could you please grab it? Bring me a drink from the printer as well," she gestured to the furthest, darkest corner of the room with her long bony hand. "I haven't spoken to anyone in a long time and my throat is getting dry."

While it was still quite difficult to see much in the room, the box that Mary retrieved appeared to be made of some sort of purple wood. Mary could only imagine how interesting the tree that it came from must have looked. The Cleric lifted the lid off of the shoebox-sized container, revealing a stack of very Earth-like looking photos.

"Now, Mary, I don't want to burden your young heart but my home world was destroyed, using your planet's time measurement system, roughly one hundred years ago. Several asteroids crashed into us, wiping everything out. The worst part is that it was avoidable," the Cleric explained while sorting through the stack of photos. "Here are some pictures of life on Photonon, before it was entirely destroyed."

"Everyone looks so...sad." Mary commented as she flipped through the all too Earth-like photographs. "Although I would be sad too, if I found out my planet was going to be destroyed."

"That is the complicated part, young Mary. They hadn't yet heard about the asteroid. Everyone was sad because they felt as if everyone hated them."

Mary was confused by this.

"Each half of the planet felt as if the other half hated them, even though they had never met. Those that felt hated chose to believe they were the victims of the other half's aggression, even though there was never any real conflict," the Cleric explained. Mary could hear a certain frustration building up in the Cleric's voice.

This situation was bizarre to Mary. She couldn't understand why anyone would believe that they were in conflict with people they had never met before. "What does this have to do with the Last Migration, though?" she asked, confused.

"Over the years, many researchers had approached decision makers with news of approaching asteroids, but the Ruling Faction always brushed the concerns off. They believed that the asteroids were too far away to be an immediate threat, and that someone else would come up with a plan later. Once the Faction realized that they had waited too long to address the problem, they gave up on governing and simply focused on filling their coffers. Our once-flourishing society began to crumble as the rich focused on hoarding resources for themselves. Some people questioned what was happening as supplies began to run out and society's morale became low, but instead of being honest about the impending destruction of the planet, our rulers decided to make citizens wary of one another as a distraction. They did this so people would compete for the remaining resources instead of working together, possibly against the Faction. Not that it would have mattered, because of the asteroids..." The Cleric leaned in and took the photos back from Mary's small hands as she continued her story. Mary could tell that the Cleric's energy was beginning to wane.

"Those of us that saw what was happening tried our best to convince people that they were being deliberately distracted, but they preferred to keep fighting amongst themselves. So much fighting, when they could have been enjoying their remaining time..."

Mary stared at the Cleric for a moment, who looked like she had fallen asleep.

"Cleric?" Mary asked, gently poking at the elderly leader's soft grey shoulder.

"I'm sorry, my mind isn't what it used to be. As I was saying… Everyone on these ships today is here because their ancestors chose to work together to save who and what we could. These ships contain every last member of our species. And thus, here we are now, traveling around and trying our best to warn other planets who are also in the path of the asteroids." The Cleric cleared her throat again. "Could you please get me another drink? I am extremely thirsty."

As Mary retrieved another drink for the Cleric, a horrible realization washed over her. "You said that you are trying to warn other planets… Is that why I am here? Are you telling me my planet is going to be destroyed too?"

The Cleric once again fell quiet.

"Is that why I am here?!" Mary asked again in a high-pitched voice that caused the Cleric to flinch.

"I am so very sorry, Mary. I didn't want to tell you, but it's my job… I really hate being the eldest. But at least one day very soon, someone else will have this role," the Cleric replied, before lowering herself back down into bed and pulling a plain white blanket up over her gaunt shoulders.

"But you said that your people have saved other planets! Why can't you save mine?" Mary pressed.

"I am very tired. I am so sorry I wasn't able to tell you what you wanted to hear, but it was very nice to meet you,

Mary. Our interaction has been the highlight of…" the Cleric trailed off. "The highlight of my life since I stopped leaving my room. You should go back to your friends. They are waiting for you down the hall. I hope that you have a good time at the conference…"

Mary wanted to continue arguing with the Cleric but noticed that she had already fallen asleep, or at the very least was pretending to have. Mary stood over her bed for a moment before walking through the sliding doors back into the bright white hallway to find Larry and Georgio.

Chapter Ten

Sunday, July 7th (1963)

The engine of George's Chevy idled loudly in the drive-way of his childhood home. The dirt road had become more craterous than the moon while dandelions and thistles peeked through cracks that had formed over the years. The house, however, looked remarkably similar, if not some how better, than when the Schmidt family lived in it. Although the house had mostly been abandoned since George moved to Penticton, he always did minor repairs during his annual trips, which was more upkeep than had been done to the house over the entire course of his childhood.

It wasn't normal for a house in Falkland to sit empty for so long, but this was a complicated situation. The house was never sold because it was still in George's mother's name. The ownership was meant to be transferred to George when he turned eighteen, but because Margaret was all but locked up, she didn't have the authority to transfer the ownership. And now here it sat in limbo, ever so slowly decaying from the outside in.

George sighed as he turned the truck off and took his keys out of the ignition. He flipped through the old key ring and found the one for the front door. Although he only returned to this place once a year, he couldn't bear to take the key off of the ring. Getting rid of the key was a step towards finally moving on from his old life that George wasn't ready to take. He grabbed his bags, hopped out of the truck and walked towards the front door, carefully checking over his shoulders to see if anyone was watching. Although the house was still technically in his mother's name, he didn't want anyone to know that he was here. It was just simpler that way.

Sure enough, a sense of panic flooded over George as soon as he walked through the front door, just as it did each year. He braced his hand against the stained wall and closed his eyes. *Breathe in, breathe out.* For a brief second, George wasn't entirely sure that he would remain conscious. The entire place was sullied with memories. Every corner, every nook, each centimetre of the house was tainted with so much history. After he finally collected himself, George set his backpack down by the front door on top of one of the mysterious stains that had been there longer than he could remember.

Out of habit, he walked towards the old refrigerator and opened it up to grab a drink. Suddenly, a centipede the length of a ruler fell out of the inner door, causing George to let out a shriek that, at best, would alert the neighbours to his presence, and at worst, make them think that a young girl was being murdered. Or eaten by a mountain lion. With the centipede already hiding somewhere else in the kitchen, George collected his thoughts and focused on why he was here in the first place: to look for his sister. Tomorrow would be the anniversary of her disappearance. Making a mental note to buy some ice to put into the fridge tomorrow, George picked up his backpack and made his way to his old bedroom where he would camp out for the night.

Chapter Eleven

Thursday, July 10th (1947) – Stardate 194707.10

"When were you going to tell me about the asteroids?!" Mary yelled down the long corridor to Georgio and Larry, who were awkwardly staring out the window while waiting for her meeting to end. The two beings flinched and covered their ear holes, which were where Mary imagined their ears would be; it was clear they were not used to dealing with loud sounds.

"It wasn't our decision to tell you," Georgio responded.

"As you just heard, our people are not good at making our own decisions because we are easily tricked. That is why we defer all important decisions to the Cleric," Larry added matter-of-factly.

"But wasn't your reliance on bad leaders what got your planet destroyed?" Mary asked, hoping her point was clear.

The two beings paused. Mary was not sure if they were communicating to each other in a way that she was unable to hear, or if they were actually thinking in silence. Made uncomfortable by the silence, she grumbled, "I don't even think the Cleric likes being in charge." She knew that it was bratty of her to imply that the Cleric was wrong, but she didn't care.

"That may be true, but she is our leader and that needs to be respected," Georgio replied in a way that made Mary feel even smaller than she was. She was just a child, why should she have expected them to listen to her? She had assumed that because of all of their technology, that the aliens would be more intelligent than humans, but yet again Mary realised that they had more in common than she would have liked.

"Our original goal was to warn your planet, but after everything that happened with you and young Ray, the Cleric thinks that it would be too risky for our people. When your population is as small as ours, each life matters even more. We can't afford to lose another ship if we want our species to continue." Larry tried his best to explain, but the pauses he took between certain words made Mary think that he wasn't really sure if he truly believed what he was saying.

"Your planet won't be at risk for another twenty or so Earth-years. It is possible that they will solve the problem on their own, without any of us being placed in danger," Georgio stated. *"Besides, why would you want to go back? When we rescued you, other humans were firing guns at you,"* he added.

"And one woman threw a shoe!" Larry added.

"Yeah, that was my mom..." Mary trailed off.

"Why would you want to save any of those humans?" Georgio pressed.

"Not everyone is bad," Mary answered. "My little brother is a good person! I need to save him."

"Your species won't listen," Larry replied.

"Maybe not to me, but they'll listen to all of you! We just won't land in Falkland, is all," Mary bargained as her energy started to wane. Based on past experiences, she knew that once she started trying to barter with adults, she had already lost the argument in their eyes. She suddenly felt so very tired. This time though, Larry and Georgio did not reply, they only continued to stare with their large doe eyes. "Please?" she asked once more, with her own wide-open pleading stare.

"Returning you to Earth is going to be challenging," Georgio finally replied.

"Why?" Mary asked, with a hint of optimism. Adults never listened to Mary; she really hadn't been expecting to change their minds!

"Time moves differently out here," Georgio tried to explain. *"We really didn't think you would want to return..."* Larry added.

"I NEED TO GO BACK!" Mary shrieked with all of her remaining might, drawing the attention of everyone in earshot on the mostly-silent ship. Each bystander in the gathering area stopped what they were doing to watch the scene. First humming, and now yelling; they were becoming quite intrigued by this small human. This made her realize that perhaps people back on Earth would listen to a nine-year-old girl, if only she was loud enough. "Please, you've got to take me home. I need to at least try."

"Okay," Georgio conceded. *"But first, since we're already here, let us show you around the conference."*

"You aren't mad at me for getting upset?" Mary asked, trying to calm down now that they had agreed to bring her back to Earth.

"Of course not. You are our friend," Larry answered. *"Friendship is boring without a difference of opinions. We don't always need to agree on everything."*

Chapter Twelve

Monday, July 8th (1963)

George stared vacantly at the calendar hanging behind the gas station's cash register. The swimsuit model for July looked as excited to be posing with the red muscle car as George was to be waiting to pay for his coffee. Her face was beautiful, sure, but George didn't believe her smile. It looked too forced. Perhaps though, he was putting too much thought into pin-up art designed to be hung at gas stations and rest stops.

"Can I help you?" the cashier asked while emerging from the storage room, chewing on too large of a piece of gum. Her tongue flicked in and out of her mouth as she tried, and failed, to blow a bubble. Her name tag read: Lucy. There was a familiarity about her that he couldn't quite put his finger on, although in a place with only several hundred people you were bound to run across someone from your past once in a while. "Just here for a cup of joe," George replied while gesturing with his beverage, which was now cold because of the ten minutes he spent waiting for the gum-chewing attendant to emerge. A lukewarm mug of gas station coffee wasn't most people's first choice, but in 1963 Falkland, the options were limited. Besides, the Schmidt house didn't have power these days.

"That coffee's pretty old, you know," Lucy answered while punching the sale into the register, still chewing on the gum as if it was cud.

"Oh, okay..." He debated asking about a new pot but felt like that would only cause trouble. *It's not as if this coffee is any worse than the free kind at work,* George mused while glancing up at the calendar again. In that moment he realized that he and the model were both just playing roles: George was the completely normal young man that hadn't secretly dedicated his life to searching for aliens, while the model was most certainly a real muscle car enthusiast.

As George slid the cashier a nickel to pay for his drink, he debated asking if she knew his sister. Although, if she had known Mary, he somehow doubted that they had been very good friends.

"Have a nice day," George said as he left the gas station, but by then Lucy was already back in the storage room. Coffee in hand, he decided to wander around Falkland for a bit as he had an entire day to kill before nightfall. Susan Webb could probably use an apology. And with that, George awkwardly went back into the Esso Gas Station to buy a second coffee to bring to his old caretaker. Hopefully he wouldn't need to wait another ten minutes.

***

At the conference, word had traveled about Mary's incredible humming skills. Rumours moved much faster and further when telepathy was involved, which resulted in Mary humming so much that her lips still felt numb the next day. She also consumed copious amounts of delicacies at the massive feast. Although there were no labels, most of the dishes appeared to be cake-like, which made it especially difficult to say no to second and third servings. One of the beings had assured her that calories didn't count during conferences and to eat as much as she wanted. Mary didn't know what a calorie was, but she was happy that no one was going to call her greedy. By the time that she returned to her quarters, Mary was too exhausted to visualize more than an extra fluffy pillow and blanket.

Just as it did on the way to the Void, the trip back to Earth only took Mary and the aliens a single day. She had no idea how they were able to traverse space so quickly, and didn't know enough about physics to even begin asking questions. Frankly, Mary wasn't even sure what physics was, or how it would relate to space, it was just a term she had seen on a classroom poster once. As she would soon find out though, there was a major difference between how time flowed during transgalactic space travel and time on Earth.

"We have entered Earth's orbit," Georgio announced while walking through the sliding door leading into Mary's quarters. *"Are you sure you want us to return you to Earth? You are welcome to stay with us, if you would like,"* Larry offered with a hint of sadness in his eyes.

"I need to go back to my brother," Mary replied, trying to hide her own emotions. Although it had only been several days, Mary had grown quite fond of Larry and Georgio.

"I understand," Georgio answered. *"Larry and I have spoken, and we have a proposal for you though. We are not able to break tradition by disobeying the Cleric, but the two of us have thought of a workaround of sorts."*

Needless to say, this piqued Mary's interest.

"Since the Cleric did not believe that saving your planet would be a worthwhile endeavour, we can't interfere ourselves. However, the Cleric didn't say that we couldn't help you *save Earth,"* Larry explained while passing Mary a piece of rolled-up paper that he had been holding. *"I have drawn you a map indicating the source and trajectory of the asteroids."*

Mary accepted the papers, but upon realizing her dress had no pockets, decided to fold them and place the map in her left shoe. The Photoneons looked at her oddly, as if they were adding this to their mental lists of weird things that humans do. Meanwhile, Mary was secretly hoping that Larry's drawings were better than the ones that he made on her food printer.

"While you find a way to give these maps to your leaders, we will remain in orbit in case you once again find yourself in trouble with the authorities," Georgio explained.

The idea of being in trouble with the authorities for a second time was amusing to Mary. She was a good kid – mostly – and yet somehow, within the matter of only a few days, she may end up having a second encounter with them.

At this rate, someone in Hollywood was going to have to make a movie about her!

"How will you know where to find me?" Mary asked.

A peripheral scan of Earth had revealed an immense growth in radio signals since they were last here; all they had to do was to constantly scan the signals for mentions of Mary. She was a small child who was going to try to tell her world's leaders about an impending asteroid shower – surely, she'd end up being recorded by someone! However, Larry kept his response simple. *"You're not one to blend in,"* he stated earnestly.

Chapter Thirteen

Monday, July 8th (1963)

Leaving a flying saucer wasn't nearly as exciting as boarding one. After all, there was no way for the return to one's hometown to be as riveting as escaping said town in a UFO and blasting off into the unknown. Mary knew exactly what would be awaiting her in Falkland: her dirty old bedroom, a mostly empty fridge, and her mother angrily pacing around the house. Mary could only imagine how furious her mom was going to be at her. She was probably going to have to spend the rest of the summer doing every chore in the house!

As Mary prepared to take the last step off of the spaceship's ramp, she turned back for one final look at Larry and Georgio. While they had assured her that they would remain in Earth's orbit and would come back as soon as she needed them, she couldn't help but worry how they would fare without her. As she had discovered, they didn't even know what music was! And with that, she sprinted back up the ramp to give them each one more hug.

"We will miss you too, Mary, but we will be united again soon," Georgio said as he leaned down and embraced Mary with his long, scaly arms.

"It's not that we want to leave you, but your people will likely attack us again if they see us," Larry added, while wrapping his slightly longer arms around Mary as well.

"I know, and I want you to all be safe," Mary replied, "but I wish I wasn't going to have to do this alone."

"You won't be alone, you'll have us, up there," Georgio explained while gesturing to the sky. The Photoneon's telepathic words felt very reminiscent of Mary's earlier promise to her little brother. Here she was now though, back on Earth as she had promised. It was hard to believe that so much had happened in only several days; Mary was going to have many stories to tell little Georgie.

Once she had climbed up the embankment of the quarry and was safely out of the ship's blast radius, the flying saucer emitted a blindingly bright blue glow and zipped back off into space. Mary looked around at the empty quarry and into the forest behind her. Everything was the same, including the warm summer weather. It was as if no time had passed at all; although she had only been in space for a few days, Mary was still expecting something to be different. She certainly *felt* different, even if Falkland itself hadn't changed. And then suddenly, Mary felt a familiar feeling as her stomach let out a ravenous grumble. Without access to an on-demand food printer, Mary realized she was going to need to find her own dinner. Suddenly, she remembered that there was still some fishing gear at her camp. She most definitely wasn't prepared to confront her mother's wrath on an empty stomach. If she hurried, there would be enough time to hopefully catch and cook up a trout before dusk. Although she had been gone for a few days, Mary still felt like her mother would be less mad at her if she were to return home before nightfall.

***

This is very strange, Mary thought to herself. After wandering around the forest for at least two hours – based on her best reading of the sun's position in the sky, anyway – Mary couldn't find her camp. It was as if the entire forest had shifted. The large trees were all in the same spots, but all of the shrubs had become overgrown, or were missing entirely. The creek was even lower than the last time she had cast a line in it. Everything was ever so slightly different. Resigned to the fact that she wasn't going to have fish for dinner, Mary felt into the tongue of her old shoe and pulled out a nickel that she had tucked in it for emergencies. She wanted to save the money for a real emergency, but now that she was actually faced with using it, Mary realized that she couldn't think of a real emergency that could be solved with a nickel. *A nickel won't help me warn everyone about the asteroids that are going to blow up the planet in twenty years.* That settled it; Mary was going to use the nickel to buy a chocolate bar for dinner.

***

The sounds of the warm summer air blowing across the arid grass of the neighbouring farmer's field and the distant chirps from crickets was music to George's ears. Although the town itself had lost its charm to him years ago, he would never grow tired of the summers in this part of the province. He laid back in his lawn chair and took a long drink from a green glass bottle before unfurling the collection of star charts he had printed at work.

Based on his best research attempts – which was how George was choosing to refer to his frequent eavesdropping on the researchers at the observatory – there might have been some irregularities spotted towards the Orion Constellation. This was as good of a lead as any! However, when George held the star chart up to the sky, his heart sank: during this time of year, the Orion Constellation was only visible from the southern hemisphere.

Now what? He thought to himself in dismay. George had hoped that this year, with the star charts, he would have more of a chance at figuring out where the aliens took Mary. But now he was back in the same situation he found him- self in every July 8th: alone in his old backyard with a case of beer, waiting for nightfall. It was beginning to feel pathetic. George popped the top of his second bottle and sank into his lawn chair.

Chapter Fourteen

What are all of these chocolate bars? Mary pondered as she strolled down the candy aisle of Falkland's only gas station. *Butterfingers, Snickers... Milky Way?* The old couple that owns the store must have brought some rare kinds up from their last trip across the border. Mary picked up a Milky Way and set it next to the cash register. Despite its name, she knew it was unlikely that it would taste anything like the cake from the Photoneon's conference but she figured it was worth a shot.

She stood at the till for several moments, unsure if the cashier was able to spot her short frame from the other side of the counter. "Hello?" Mary called out.

"Hold your horses. Everyone in this town is so impatient," the cashier muttered while wrapping up whatever her important task was, and turning around to ring through the chocolate bar. "That'll be six cents."

"Six cents? For chocolate?" Mary asked, perturbed. Chocolate bars were usually just one cent, and she only had a nickel. "Hey, take it up with Prime Minister Pearson," the cashier snarked while chewing on a massive gob of bubble gum. For a brief moment, her eyes locked with Mary's and, perhaps sensing something familiar about her, softened her tone. "But I'll sell it to you for a nickel this time. Just don't tell the owners."

"Thank you," Mary replied gratefully. She noticed the cashier's name tag: Lucy. "Did you just move here?" Mary asked.

"Nah, I grew up here," Lucy replied. "You remind me of someone," Mary said.

"You remind me of someone too, kid," Lucy added. "Anyway, enjoy your chocolate bar. I've got to make some more coffee before all of the drivers stop here after work."

Mary walked out of the gas station and took a bite of the Milky Way bar. It was delicious, like chocolate always was, but something about the entire interaction made Mary feel wary. At least she was now able to go home with a full stomach.

***

At long last, the sun began to ever so slightly dip in the horizon. It wouldn't officially be nightfall for several hours, but at least the sun was no longer shining right onto George's face. Sure, he could have taken shelter in the house until nightfall, but that wasn't his tradition. Every year, rain or shine, George kept his promise to himself that he would wait in this exact spot to see if Mary returned, and every year, he did just that. In his lower moments, George felt stupid for even trying. These low moments were usually experienced the next day when George would be inspecting his terrible sunburns.

What are the odds that Mary will return on this exact day, in this exact spot? Thoughts about giving up would cross his mind, but he usually chose to numb that feeling with alcohol. Part of him worried that if Mary did return and did see him in this state, that she would be embarrassed of who he became, which only led to him drinking more. These feelings were why he only allowed himself to drink on weekends. Sure, today was a Monday but George rationalized that, because he had taken the day off from work, it counted as a weekend. George paused for a moment in reflection: maybe he had a drinking problem after all...

***

"How odd," Mary muttered to herself as she approached her house. Was the gravel driveway somehow worse? Or was the house slightly better? Something had changed, but Mary couldn't quite put her finger on it. Maybe whoever drove the futuristic-looking truck that was parked in the driveway could tell her what was happening.

As she approached the front door, a nervousness washed over Mary. The last time she was here, her mother's boyfriend had killed the young Photoneon, Ray, which led to this entire ordeal in the first place. Even though her mom was the one who dated that psychopath, Mary knew that her mother was going to be livid with her as soon as she walked through those doors. She took a deep breath and reminded herself that there was more at stake right now than whether or not she was going to get yelled at. Mary needed to keep her promise to her brother, and somehow alert the leaders of the world that Earth was most likely going to be destroyed by asteroids in twenty or so years. Logically, she knew her mother's rage wasn't actually important in this moment, but Mary still began to feel anxious.

I guess I've got to rip this off like a Band-Aid, Mary thought to herself as she took one more deep breath, before trying to open the door. *Wait. Who locked it?* No one ever locked their doors in Falkland, even a family as untrusting as the Schmidt's would only lock their doors when they went out of town. Mary was going to have to try to climb in through her bedroom window!

She stood at the bottom of the window for several minutes, unsure of how to get up. It was easy enough to climb down out of a window, but climbing up was much more challenging, especially without Georgie to help. *Where is everyone? And whose truck is out front?* After several attempts at jumping up, Mary was at last able to grab on to the outside of the window frame, only to discover that her bedroom window was locked too! *Did they go on a trip without me?* The thought of her family going out of town without her momentarily upset Mary, before she remembered that she had gone into the furthest part of the galaxy without them. Assuming that she was in fact going to be locked out for a few days, Mary began to wish that she had saved half of that chocolate bar. At least she'd be able to sleep in the late Friedrich's old tin shed out back.

***

Several beers later, George felt his eyes start to get heavy. The alcohol, combined with the intense summer heat, was making it extremely difficult to stay awake. Staring into the sky without any other form of entertainment also wasn't the most captivating. As the warm embrace of sleep began to wash over him, George noticed something rustling in the farmer's field. Perhaps a deer?

***

While rounding the corner of the house and into the backyard, Mary spotted someone sitting in a lawn chair. Did her mom get a new boyfriend already? Stranger things had happened, Mary supposed. Perhaps they also owned the truck out front. Mary considered walking straight up to him to ask, before another thought crossed her mind. What if he was one of the agents that had chased her into the flying saucer? What if he had arrested her entire family, and was now waiting to arrest her too?! Mary began to panic. She debated running back into the woods as she had done many times before. This time though, Mary knew she needed to be brave. She was on a mission, and sure as sun wasn't going to let everyone down. Deciding to implement the first plan that she thought of, Mary sneakily grabbed a shovel from Friedrich's old shed, and brought it with her as she snuck up behind the individual in the lawn chair. She knew she'd never be strong enough to fight a grown man, but thought that the shovel would at least make her seem more intimidating, in case he gave her any guff.

***

So what if there's a deer in the field, who cares, George thought to himself as his eyes grew even heavier. Catching himself just before his eyelids sealed shut, George shook himself awake and set the timer on his wristwatch. There, now he could have a few minutes of shut-eye without getting as sun burnt as last time. He didn't need to worry about some silly deer rummaging about. Just as he finally gave into the idea of sleep, George swore it looked as if the distant figure was walking on two legs. Before he could be certain though, George's eyes finally shut.

***

As Mary crept closer to the man in the lawn chair, she noticed someone way out in the farmer's field: the farmer! She hadn't seen him around in quite some time and gave him a friendly wave. This was Mary's effort to be neighbourly and also her way of ensuring that she had a witness as she confronted the possible secret agent. Rather than waving back though, the farmer stared at Mary as if he had seen a ghost. Mary waved again. Nothing. The farmer suddenly began sprinting back to his house as fast as his elderly legs could take him. *Oh no,* Mary thought to herself, *they've gotten to him too!*

She gripped the shovel tightly as she approached the man in the lawn chair.

"Excuse me, sir?" Mary spoke softly while using the shovel to nudge the stranger who had apparently dozed off in the lawn chair. When her gentle pokes did nothing to rouse the stranger, she turned the shovel around and used the handle to poke him straight in the belly. This definitely woke him up.

"What in tarnation?!" George sputtered out, taken aback by the sudden intrusion. He wasn't expecting to wake up to someone jabbing him in the gut! His eyes struggled to adjust to the bright sunlight.

"Who are you and where is my family?" Mary demanded, brandishing the shovel as menacingly as she could.

"M-M...M...Mary?" George stuttered, wondering if he was hallucinating. He knew in that moment that he needed to lay off the sauce.

"Yes, I'm Mary. Now who are you?! Don't make me ask a third time!" Mary threatened while continuing to hold the shovel high above her head, which was proving exceedingly difficult to keep up. She wasn't one to act violent like this, even though she had vaporized – or rather, gooified – her abusive stepfather with a ray gun. Mary considered herself to be a pacifist. Most nine-year-olds weren't familiar with that term, but Mary read the word in a *National Geographic* once and it sounded nice to her. Regardless, she had never brandished a shovel at someone before, and had no idea it would be so difficult to do for longer than a few seconds.

"Mary, it's me!" George said while reaching towards the shovel which Mary lowered without resistance as her arms were extremely tired.

"Who is 'me'?" Mary pressed. She had no idea who this strange man was.

"I'm George!" he said as a great joy washed over his face. Mary stared at this man who claimed to be Georgie. The Georgie she remembered was a chubby little toddler with ash blonde hair and a pale face. This grown adult had freckles and chestnut hair. This couldn't be her little Georgie. She stared for a moment longer though, and realized that he looked exactly like their father did in old wedding pictures. For the first time in her life, Mary was truly speechless.

"It's been so long, Mary. I have missed you so, so, so much," George said, holding back tears as he wrapped his adult-sized arms around Mary's small frame. Mary wasn't sure how to respond to the discovery that her little brother had aged nearly twenty years in a week, so she simply hugged him back.

Chapter Fifteen

Mary stared up at her fully grown little brother who was now sitting across from her at the kitchen table. How did this happen? She couldn't understand how time had progressed so much faster on Earth than it had when she was in space. Is this what Larry and Georgio tried to warn her about when she begged to return?

"Georgie, I am so sorry. I promised you I would come back. I… I tried to come home as fast as I could," Mary explained while choking back tears. "I thought I was only gone for a few days."

"I waited for you for sixteen years," George confessed. "For you it was only a few days, but for me it was a lifetime." Although his big sister was now bizarrely his little sister, he felt incredibly small in this moment.

Mary scanned the kitchen; other than the table and refrigerator, the entire room was bare. She had already caught a glance of the appalling state of her old bedroom, which was also empty except for George's sleeping bag and a few posters he had hung up as a teenager and never removed. George's teddy bear, Mr. Purdy, all of their books, all of their toys…

Everything familiar from Mary's childhood had been packed away. "Where is Mom?" Mary finally asked.

***

George explained everything that had happened following Mary's alien abduction as they drove to Dellview to visit Margaret. Visiting hours would almost be over at this point, but they needed to try. Their mother would never forgive either of them if George waited to tell her about Mary's return.

As they sped along the Trans Canada Highway, George caught Mary up on the last sixteen years. He explained how the town turned against their mother and how she was consequently committed to a mental institution after Mary disappeared, and how he was made to live with Susan Webb for a brief period before being allowed to move back home alone.

Mary used to think that her old teacher was one of the best people in the entire world, but after hearing the stories of how she would call Georgie by their father's name, and how Ms. Webb was so convinced Mary was eaten by wildlife, her opinion shifted. "I would never let a bear eat me!" Mary had blurted out indignantly during that part of the story. After meeting with the reluctant Cleric, and now hearing these stories, Mary was developing a less than favourable opinion of adults. *Although, Georgie is an adult now too,* she silently considered. It was all a lot to take in.

For all of the seriousness of their conversation, Mary had enjoyed the drive with George. He drove quite fast and liked to speed around other drivers on the highway, which Mary found fun. She couldn't help but picture him piloting a flying saucer alongside Georgio and Larry. Somehow there wasn't a long enough lull in the conversation for Mary to tell George about her friends from Photonon, but since it was going to be close to another twenty years for the asteroids to impact Earth, Mary decided she could catch George up on her space adventure later.

As George's truck pulled into Dellview's parking lot, Mary was overcome with a feeling of dread. She could only imagine how angry her mom would be with her – she was definitely going to be grounded for the rest of the summer! Mary held her breath as she hopped out of the Chevy, breathing again only once her small feet landed on the concrete.

"Before we go in there, you need to prepare yourself," George said, trying to sound as adult as he could muster.

"I know Georgie, I know! She's going to ground me!" Mary replied.

"Mom's not going to ground you," George answered, at first shocked by the obliviousness of Mary's concern before remembering again that, in Mary's mind, it had been less than a week since she last saw their mother. "You need to prepare yourself for the shock of seeing Mom in her current state."

"Current state?"

"Mom's had a rough sixteen years. She's a lot older now. And much frailer. You don't need to be afraid of her."

Mary couldn't fathom seeing her mom as anything other than tough. What would this new version of Mom look like?

Had she traded her jeans for a frilly dress? Was her room in Dellview decorated with doilies and throw pillows?

As George prepared to go into Dellview, he caught himself hesitating outside of the front entrance just as he always did. For a moment, he wondered if Mary noticed his anxiety towards the hospital, but as he looked down, he noticed Mary was also beginning to pace. George paused for a moment and realized that while they both had bad memories from their childhood, Mary needed him to be the adult right now. George knelt down to her height before telling her, "We'll go through the doors together, on the count of three." George took Mary's hand as he stood back up. "One, two, three—" he said as he walked bravely through the front door of the facility, hand in hand with Mary.

"Oh! I didn't know you had a daughter!" an annoying voice called out, interrupting George's brief moment of pride.

"Hi Tammy," George replied with a sigh. "She even looks like you!" Tammy gushed.

"Oh no, ma'am. I'm his sist—" Mary was quickly interrupted by George kicking the back of her foot.

"She's got my sense of humour too," George replied to Tammy with an awkward forced chuckle and a wink. "Come on, let's go see Grandma Margaret," he mumbled while taking Mary by the hand and leading her away from Nurse Tammy.

"What was that about?" Mary asked.

"Do you remember what I said about Ms. Webb thinking you were eaten by a bear?"

"Yes?" Mary tried to contain the annoyance she felt by someone implying she was anything less than a great outdoors man.

"Well, *everyone* except for Mom and I think you were eaten by wildlife."

"Everyone thinks I am dead?" Mary couldn't believe she needed to say those words out loud.

"No one believed you went to space. They just assumed Mom went crazy, which you've got to admit, was kind of inevitable," George admitted.

"But what about the policemen? Everyone saw me go in the spaceship!" Mary exclaimed as they approached Margaret's bedroom door.

"It's a long story," George answered. "Just, brace yourself, okay? And try to be patient. Mom is… different now," George looked at Mary in a way that implied that for the rest of their time at Dellview, she should take his lead.

Mary stood outside of her mother's bedroom door and did her best to prepare herself to see the woman who, the last time they interacted, threw a shoe at her through a hail of police gunfire. For all intents and purposes, Mary knew Margaret had her own reasons for the things she did, but much of what she did was frightening for a child. Or any reasonable adult. Mary loved her mom, but she didn't like her.

Just then, through the thin care home door, Mary overheard George explaining to their mother that he had brought someone she should see. Taking this as her cue, Mary walked into the room.

"Hi, Mom," Mary spoke softly, overcome with sadness as she took in her mom's new appearance. Her strong frame had become much thinner. Skinny, even. Her strong arms that, on good days, used to drag Mary around the house in a laundry basket or push her on the tire swing, were now weak and sinewy. Her once dark chestnut hair was now streaked with grey. Unsure of how to handle this, Mary instinctively reached towards Margaret for a hug. She wasn't expecting her mother to take two steps back.

"Is this a joke?" Margaret sputtered. She barely gave Mary a second glance. "George, did one of the nurses put you up to this? What sort of sick twisted person are you?"

"Mom!" George pleaded. "It really is Mary." Mary didn't move.

"Mary abandoned us nearly twenty years ago. This child. This… thing. This isn't Mary," Margaret stammered.

"Mom, it really is me!" Mary said loudly. "I was only gone for a few days, but somehow, it was longer for you. I am so sorry! I didn't mean to leave for so long!"

"George, I don't think I can handle this right now. Perhaps you should come back later, without *her*," Margaret shot back. Her body had gotten weak, but the venom in her tone was just as potent as Mary remembered.

"Mom," Mary pled, choking back tears. George placed his hand on her shoulder.

"Let's go, Mary," George said while turning to leave.

Suddenly, Mary was overcome with a feeling of defiance. She didn't travel all of the way across the Milky Way and back again only to be made sad by her mean mother. "You don't have to believe me, but it's me. I'm real. I came all of the way back to save you and Georgie!"

"Wait, to save us?" George asked.

"I wanted to tell you earlier," Mary confessed. "But you had so many stories, I figured I could wait."

"What do you want to save us from? Life?" Margaret replied with one of her trademarked sarcastic eye rolls as she proceeded to light a cigarette.

"You smoke now?" Mary asked, disgustedly.

"It's been a long sixteen years, kid," Margaret retorted in a way that made Mary realize that her mom hadn't changed quite as much as George had implied. The way she said 'sixteen years' started to rattle around in Mary's head.

"Georgie... what year did you say it was?" Mary asked.

"Nineteen-sixty-three," George answered.

"And what year did I go to space?" Mary asked, counting on her small fingers.

"Nineteen-forty-seven?" George replied, growing confused.

"And that is sixteen years..." Mary trailed off. "Oh no," she mumbled as she made a dark discovery. "Please, please don't be mad, but I'm supposed to tell everyone about some asteroids that are approaching. I thought I had years before we needed to worry, but now I'm realizing that we might be running out of time..." Mary was so embarrassed. She had only just finished third grade; it wasn't fair for adults to expect this much out of her.

"Let's go, we'll talk in the truck," George said while leading Mary out of Margaret's room.

"You never were good at math, were you," Margaret called out before taking a deep puff of her cigarette.

Mary knew her mother remembered everything.

Chapter Sixteen

George watched over Mary as she napped in his bed, hugging his old teddy Mr. Purdy. He didn't have much left from their childhood, and was thankful to be able to give her this small comfort after the horrible meeting with their mother. Mary's chest rose up and down as she breathed deeply, taking in the warm summer air. The apartment windows were wide open, allowing the hot breeze to flood the small bachelor pad. When they arrived back at his apartment in Penticton, Mary was adamant that she couldn't nap. Quickly taking on his newly assigned big brother role though, George insisted that she lay down for just five minutes; if she didn't fall asleep during that time, he was going to take her out for ice cream. Mary tossed and turned for the first two minutes, most likely wanting to stay awake simply to win the bet, but by the third minute, she was out like a hibernating bear.

Mary had explained everything to George on their drive back to Penticton. It wasn't too long of a drive, but Mary, like many nine-year-old girls, could speak really fast when she needed to. She explained everything she knew about the asteroids and the space conference, as well as stories about her new friends, Larry and Georgio. George really hoped he would get to meet them one day too. Now though, as his sister slept, George was trying to figure out how exactly they were going to warn everyone about the potential asteroid impact. The most obvious solution was to tell Robert and the others at the observatory – surely they would know what to do with the information. But George knew if he did that, and Mary had the information wrong, that they'd never trust him with anything again. They'd think that George was a loon, just like his mother. Everything he had worked for over the past several years would turn out to have been for nothing. As he watched Mary though, it finally clicked that he had achieved his goals. Finding Mary was the reason that he had pursued a career in space research in the first place, and now, here she was. Technically she had found him, but that didn't seem to matter at this point. The entire experience was surreal and it was going to take a while for everything to sink in.

Despite all of this, he still felt anxious about the notion of speaking up at work. Yes, Mary was back. But what was he going to do next? If Mary was wrong, or if his team at work simply didn't want to listen to him, he'd be out on the streets. How could he pay his rent and care for his little sister if he didn't have a job? Speaking of caring for little sisters, he wasn't even sure what little girls ate, other that ice cream. He was going to need to cook proper meals! This was all a lot of pressure for someone shy of twenty years old. Suddenly, Mary began to stir.

***

Mary awoke with a start as she noticed George sitting on the corner of the bed. *Where am I?* It took a moment for Mary to remember as the post-nap fog faded from her vision. She looked down and discovered that she was still hugging Mr. Purdy. It meant a lot to her that George had hung on to some things from their childhood all of this time.

"Can we still go for ice cream?" Mary asked, rubbing the sleep from her eyes.

***

Walking along the Okanagan Lake shoreline, Mary began to notice all of the small changes that had happened in the past sixteen years. Clothes were more vibrant, and much shorter. She was surprised to see young women walking around in cropped tops, but figured the fashion changes made sense, especially given the summer heat. What shocked her the most though, was the way that people wearing something called "roller skates" would whip by her and her brother. George assured her that these contraptions – wheeled metal attachments that strapped on to the bottom of shoes – had existed for some time. But Mary hadn't seen those before, certainly not having grown up in Falkland.

"Are we going to talk to the scientists after this?" Mary asked, halfway through her chocolate ice cream cone.

"I…" George began. How desperately he wanted to be honest and to tell her that he was scared too, but with the reversal of their age gap, it felt weird to dump his emotions on to her.

"You didn't finish your sentence," Mary spoke up as she crunched on the remaining piece of waffle cone.

George scanned the beach and for the first time, really noticed how many families were out enjoying the sun. It reminded him of when he bought his red truck and then couldn't help but notice just how many other red vehicles were on the road. While he was usually focused on himself, or looking for other people his age, this time out he was incredibly aware of how many children there were. How many children that were kind and smart and full of potential, just like Mary. He thought about his life as he knew it and the respect that he wanted to gain from the scientists at work and had the stark realization that none of it would mean anything if the world was wiped out by asteroids.

"I'm scared, Mary," George confessed.

"I am too, Georgie," Mary replied, taking her brother's hand. "But you need to be brave, like when we…" Mary paused for a moment. "Like when you were little." It struck the both of them in that moment how much the dynamics of their relationship had changed.

"I learned something when I was in space," Mary started to explain. "Sometimes people only do the things they think they're supposed to do, because it is easier, even if it's wrong.

They don't want others to get mad at them or to think they are silly, so they stay quiet instead of trying to do the right thing."

"Did Larry and Georgio teach you that?" George asked, impressed at how wise she had grown.

"They did, but I don't think they meant to," Mary answered. "I realized on my own that if the first Photoneon hadn't crashed in Falkland, then the aliens never would have met me. And maybe they never would have found someone that would listen to them."

"That is a very good point," George said. "You know, if you hadn't disappeared, I wouldn't have started working at the observatory. And then, who would be able to warn everyone?"

"Does that mean you're going to tell them?" Mary asked.

"It means we're going to tell them, together."

Chapter Seventeen

Tuesday, July 9th (1963)

"Thank you to everyone who came here to listen to me today," George stated as clearly as he could to the room full of scientists. Technically there were only two scientists, his colleague Robert, and another researcher, Chris, who was closer to George's age, but it was a small room. "I have something of great importance that I need to talk with you about today." George pretended he couldn't notice the odd way that Robert was looking at him.

"What exactly is this about, son?" Robert asked with concern.

"Don't you handle my printing?" Chris added, with an air of judgement.

"Yes sir, that's me," George mumbled, his confidence started to wane as thoughts of self-doubt washed over him. *What am I doing? I'm going to lose my job. Mary might be wrong, and then what? No, I need to do this. This is the right thing to do.* He paused for a moment and cleared his throat before continuing. "I'm sorry, I just get nervous speaking to actual real scientists."

"Take all of the time you need," Robert offered, "I'm salary."

"Are you quitting?" Chris asked.

"I'm here because I have some very important news, and you are the only people that can help," George explained while taking Mary's map out of his back pocket. As he unfolded it, he prayed that the scientists wouldn't notice that it smelled like a dirty foot. "I have it under great authority that Earth is going to be hit by asteroids sometime soon. Maybe today, maybe in a few years, but soon."

"Was that drawn by someone's kid?" Chris asked, as if he was a character written only to progress a plot line.

George looked down at the drawing and sighed. "I can see why you might think that… But I assure you that this picture is of extraterrestrial origin." And with that, George could tell that both Robert and Chris thought he was entirely insane. Feeling beads of sweat form on his forehead, George pivoted to his second plan. "You know what, there is someone else you should speak to. She'll be better at this than me. Hang on," George gestured as he left the small room to retrieve Mary, who was waiting in a neighbouring office.

"Does she work for the National Research Council?" Chris called out.

"No, but she has been to space," George stated while leading Mary around the corner.

"NASA?" Robert questioned.

"Not exactly…" George wiped the sweat from his forehead with his sleeve.

"Hi," Mary replied with a single wave. She hated being the centre of attention, but after everything she had gone through over the past several days, this awkward moment felt like small potatoes. She took the map out of George's hand, and did her best to explain Larry's drawings which unfortunately were as messy as she had assumed. "So, I don't know the details, but my friends from Photonon have outlined everything in this drawing. See, if you look here," Mary gestured to a scribble, "that's where the asteroids originated. And here, that is where Photonon was, before it was destroyed."

"This kid is like Joseph Smith," Chris whispered sarcastically to Robert, who was having the opposite reaction and was in fact stunned by the entire ordeal.

"George… I thought you had a big sister? Who is this child?" Robert asked.

"Robert, I would like you to meet my big sister, Mary," George said while motioning to Mary. "She didn't die sixteen years ago, she was abducted by aliens. I know that sounds insane, but well, here she is."

"I was actually only gone for a week, but they took me to an intergalactic conference and then there was a time warp, or something…" Mary rambled enthusiastically. "They didn't want to help us at first, but I convinced them, and then one of them called Larry made this drawing…" She trailed off as she realized that yes, in fact, her story sounded extraordinarily outlandish, no matter how true it was.

"You'll have to give me a moment," Robert said as he braced himself on the corner of his desk. "This is a lot for an old man to take in." George and Mary stared at Robert, waiting for him to collect his thoughts. Mary couldn't understand why he was hesitating to believe the situation, after all, she was clearly very real.

"Robert, you aren't actually falling for this grift, are you?" Chris, the perpetual question asker, asked.

"You clearly haven't paid attention since you started working here, but George has been busting his butt around this place. I think the least we can do is to listen to him," Robert replied. "Please, pass me the drawing would you, Mary?" Robert examined the map closely. His eyes winced, George hoped it was because he needed stronger glasses and not because of the smell of the paper. Once Earth was saved, he was going to have a serious talk with his sister about not keeping important documents in her shoes.

After a few moments, Robert finally looked back at Mary. "I believe you."

***

Countless papers and star charts were scattered across Robert's desk. "Now, Mary, I'm not sure how much you know about our research here, but the team and I track anomalous solar occurrences, among many other things..."

Mary listened intently, eager to understand more about space. Although she had literally traversed the entire Milky

Way, she knew very little about science and wanted to learn more.

"Your map lines up with a pet theory of mine... Yes, the sun is a sphere and technically we should be able to see what's happening on the other side of it, but I have a sneaking suspicion that its rays are blocking something," Robert explained. "If we are both correct, then we will need to act fast to stop the asteroids."

"How hard can it be? Can't we just shoot them down?" Mary asked, thinking about how her stepfather used to hunt gophers in the farmer's field.

"Anything to do with space is a bit more complicated than that. You've got to consider gravity, Earth's atmosphere, the amount of fuel needed to launch a rocket in the first place, not to mention the geopolitical implications—" Robert paused, noticing Mary's confusion at the last two words. "We don't want another country to think that we are trying to fire rockets at them."

Mary nodded. She supposed that made sense. "What can we do then?"

"We need more time. Having only a handful of years isn't enough to solve this on our own. But since we can't change that, we're going to need some outside help." Robert turned to George. "I need you to get my address book out of the top of my desk. Call the number written on the back page, it will connect you to the National Research Council's head office in Ottawa. Tell them that we need to hold an emergency meeting."

George nodded, and did as he was told. It was the first time that he felt like he was a true part of the team, and although he was still afraid of the idea of Earth's imminent destruction, he noticed he was smiling.

"You need to understand something, Mary. A year can feel like a million when you're young, but it's really not much time at all. Especially for scientists. In fact, we are currently running several studies that won't give us results for decades. Most of us will be retired or dead by the time the data comes in," Robert explained.

"Why do you do it then?" Mary asked, enjoying that an adult was actually speaking with her as an equal.

Robert paused for a moment. "We do it for everyone in the future. For our kids, our grandkids, their future kids... Humanity keeps going even when an individual doesn't," he concluded with a shrug.

Chapter Eighteen

Friday, September 20th (1963)

After a whirlwind two months of traveling back and forth between the Okanagan and the National Research Council's head office in Ottawa, Ontario, Mary hardly had time to come to terms with having left Earth in the first place, let alone now being responsible for saving it. And now, here she was in New York City of all places, to witness the USA's President, John F. Kennedy, give his address at the United Nations' 18th General Assembly. While she hadn't had much free time to spend with Larry and Georgio since they returned to Earth – they had located her based off radio transmissions between researchers and landed a few days ago – she was eager to see them more once the whole ordeal of saving the planet was settled. At least now, a plan was in place.

Once the tensions between several countries were eased – which was the purpose of this speech – scientists from both Canada and the United States planned to work together, through something known as the Apollo program, to shoot down the asteroids. As Robert explained to her, the public would never be allowed to learn about the existential threats of the asteroids, it was just too scary. And since missile launches would be quite hard to hide, a plan was made to incorporate the destruction of the asteroids into a preexisting plan to go to the moon. Having attached his name to several key reports, and having the most seniority, Robert had been made the key liaison between Mary, the Photoneons, and the National Research Council of Canada.

Seated in the front row, just behind a group of reporters, Mary looked around at the rows of dignitaries from around the world. While the hordes of travelers outside of New York's Idlewild Airport had quickly made her used to large crowds of people, being in a room with all of the world's leaders made her feel uneasy. There was no reason for Mary to assume that the plan to destroy the asteroids wouldn't work out, and yet she couldn't help but feel like everyone would blame her if it failed. She took comfort in having her friends with her though, and smiled up at the two Photoneons who were standing behind President Kennedy as he gave his speech.

"Ladies and gentlemen... Humans, as a species, have always been explorers, driven by an insatiable curiosity. I stand before you today to make an extraordinary announcement that will shape the course of our future... Twenty-four months ago, when I last had the honor of addressing this body, the shadow of fear lay darkly across the world..."

As John F. Kennedy addressed the crowd, Mary couldn't help but notice men in black suits who watched the reporters with suspicion. She couldn't tell for certain, but it looked as if some were having their recording equipment confiscated, specifically the ones that were filming the Photoneons.

"Today though, I am confident that we have entered a new era, an era where the reach and knowledge of our species will grow beyond the limits of our imagination. The National Aeronautics and Space Administration, in collaboration with the National Research Council of Canada, has encountered a civilization far older and more advanced than our own. The species, known as Photoneons, which hail from the planet of Photonon, have extended a hand of friendship, seeking to forge bonds of understanding and cooperation with our world. It is my sincerest desire that this proposal of cooperation from the Photoneons will also act as a unifier between Western Nations and the Soviet Union, and eventually the entire world. ... If the Soviet Union and the United States, with all of their global interests and clashing commitments of ideology, and with nuclear weapons still aimed at each other today, can find areas of common interest and agreement, then surely other nations can do the same — nations caught in regional conflicts, in racial issues, or in the death throes of old colonialism. Chronic disputes which divert precious resources from the needs of the people or drain the energies of both sides serve the interests of no one — and the badge of responsibility in the modern world is a willingness to seek peaceful solutions..."

Mary's attention drifted to Larry, who was once again fidgeting with his bejeweled sleeves. She was disappointed to have not been offered her old ceremonial robe back, but understood George's suggestion that she should blend in with the crowd.

At least she was wearing one of her several new outfits – with pockets, mind you.

"Our conflicts, to be sure, are real. Our concepts of the world are different. No service is performed by failing to make clear our disagreements. However, this is a time that calls for unity, for collaboration, and for the triumph of our shared humanity with the Photoneons. I understand that an announcement of this magnitude might be frightening to many of you, but rest assured, these beings are peaceful. ... I would say to the leaders of the Soviet Union, and to their people, that if either of our countries are to be fully secure, we need a much better weapon than the H-bomb – a weapon better than ballistic missiles or nuclear submarines – and that better weapon is peaceful cooperation Finally, in a field where the United States and the Soviet Union have a special capacity – in the field of space – there is room for new cooperation... Space offers no problems of sovereignty; by resolution of this Assembly, the members of the United Nations have foresworn any claim to territorial rights in outer space or on celestial bodies, and declared that international law and the United Nations Charter will apply. Why, therefore, should man's first flight to the moon be a matter of national competition? Why should the United States and the Soviet Union, in preparing for such expeditions, become involved in immense duplications of research, construction, and expenditure? Surely we should explore whether the scientists and astronauts of our two countries – indeed of all the world – cannot work together..."

"It's a shame that the world won't hear all of this," one of the reporters whispered to another.

"A real shame indeed, I just hope I get my camera back when those men are done with it," the other reporter replied with a defeated tone to his voice.

"The contest will continue – the contest between those who see a monolithic world and those who believe in diversity – but it should be a contest in leadership and responsibility instead of destruction, a contest in achievement instead of intimidation. Speaking for the United States of America, I welcome such a contest. For we believe that truth is stronger than error – and that freedom is more enduring than coercion. And in the contest for a better life, all the world can be a winner."

The pageantry of this event confused Mary. Several cameras flashed as Kennedy spoke, although many of them didn't even have film in them. Mary wondered if regular people would ever find out the entire truth.

"But peace does not rest in charters and covenants alone. It lies in the hearts and minds of all people. And if it is cast out there, then no act, no pact, no treaty, no organization can hope to preserve it without the support and the wholehearted commitment of all people. So let us not rest all our hopes on parchment and on paper; let us strive to build peace, a desire for peace, a willingness to work for peace, in the hearts and minds of all our people... Before I conclude, I would be remiss if I did not acknowledge the remarkable contributions of the young Mary Schmidt."

The mention of her name made Mary's cheeks turn a bright shade of red. *We knew you could do it!* Larry and Georgio both communicated to her from behind the president, as George reached over and held his sister's hand. "Mom is proud of you, too," he whispered. Whether this was actually true or not was irrelevant; it felt comforting to hear. Margaret had been invited to the assembly, but since being released from Dellview, she was uneasy about traveling very far.

"We owe her a debt of gratitude for facilitating this historic encounter. Thank you, Mary Schmidt. In closing, let us all celebrate not just the accomplishments of an institution like NASA, but also the brilliance and ingenuity of our young minds, whose potential knows no bounds. My fellow inhabitants of this planet: Let us take our stand here in this Assembly of nations. And let us see if we, in our own time, can move the world to a just and lasting peace. Thank you, and may God bless you all."

As John F. Kennedy stepped away from the podium, an immense feeling of hope washed over Mary. She didn't know much about politicians — other than a famous crude quote which compared them to diapers — but she liked President Kennedy's words. As the reporters packed up their equipment and the other delegates began to slowly leave the room, George placed his hand on her shoulder. The two of them walked hand in hand to their next meeting, where they were to debrief everything that had happened between when Mary left in 1947 and now.

While both George and Mary had been looking forward to meeting President Kennedy, the only people waiting for them in the room were Robert, Larry, and Georgio. "Please close the door," Robert asked the moment they stepped into the room. Mary could feel a tension in the room.

"It should go without saying, but the general public will never know of the Photoneons or your travels to space," Robert spoke solemnly. "Like with the asteroids, neither the Canadian or American governments feel that regular every day people can handle something as big as life off of our little rock."

"But what about the speech we just watched?" Mary asked.

"We were there for the other political leaders to see," Georgio explained.

"Hence the ceremonial robes," Larry elaborated with a disapproving head shake.

"Perhaps one day the truth will come out, but that is out of our hands," Robert added.

"How can I go back to regular life after all of this?" Mary asked with the maturity of someone who had actually aged at least sixteen years.

"That's why we are all here right now," Robert spoke softly, looking to George and then to Mary.

"Mary Schmidt, we would like to request your service onboard our ship as an official Ambassador of Earth," Georgio managed to wheeze out, in spoken word.

"I would be honoured," Mary answered, "But I have one request," she added while taking her brother's hand and holding it tightly in hers. "This time, George needs to join me."

ACKNOWLEDGEMENTS

Thank you to the following individuals for assisting with research: Steven Leclair, National Research Council Archives Office; Philippe Ouellette, National Research Council ATIP Coordinator; and Natalina Mariani, the Coordinator of Access to Information and Privacy at the Canadian Space Agency.

I would also like to give a massive heartfelt thank you to Chorong Kim, Pip Wallace, Tanya Gust, and Graeme Good, for all of your support over the years. Without people like you in my life, I wouldn't have been able to create as much as I have.

MARY & THE ALIENS contains quotes from John F. Kennedy's UN Address at the 18th United Nations Assembly which were sourced from the John F. Kennedy Presidential Library and Museum:

Kennedy, John F. "President's Speeches: UN Address, 20 September 1963, 1963: 19 September-11 October." *John F. Kennedy Presidential Library and Museum,* https://www.jfklibrary.org/asset-viewer/ archives/jfknsf-305-020

ABOUT THE AUTHOR

Ashley Good is a Canadian author and filmmaker. Her other work includes the novel, JUST ADD WATER, as well as the indie feature film, PITY PARTY (2018). She currently lives in Southern Alberta with her husband and son.

To learn more about her work, visit AshleyGood.ca.